# JUNGLE EYES

# LINDSAY MARIE MILLER

# Chapter 1

It was the latter part of spring, when a party of New England men, both young and old alike, decided to depart on a voyage across the Atlantic, in search of new island territories that had yet to be discovered. The year was 1899, and with the turn of the century at hand, there was an ever-present longing to depart from New York, if just for a season, so that all the men may come back with a feeling of accomplished exploration and adventure. The more danger present, the more thankful they would all feel towards their dear city upon their return.

The party totaled twenty-six men, with the youngest being of noble breed and family, as he was the eldest heir of Philip Rochester, a descendant of British royalty, whose ancestors had traveled to the New World and later triumphed in their victory over the red coats. His name was Henry Rochester, and at the age of twenty-five, he had yet to marry, nor express a desire to do so. In fact, the women he had come in contact with often bored him first, then drove him to leave the room without saying a word. His mother had made a point of arranging several young beauties to call upon the family nearly every week. In response, Henry made sure to have prescheduled fishing and hunting trips with his close companion, Charles Gallagher.

Charles was nearly thirty, though also remained a bachelor. With his red-orange curls and honey brown eyes, he looked exotic, his face bearing the resemblance of a striking wild fox. It was this mysterious, attractive aesthetic of Charles's appearance that allowed him to persuade many others so very easily, which had been the exact method he used when convincing Henry to join him in the first place.

"Let's go on this grand adventure," he beckoned to Henry, while they shared a bottle of wine after dinner on the eve of the Atlantic voyage.

"What's the point, Charlie?" Henry placed his fingers around the wine glass, bringing the red liquid to his lips, merely because there was nothing else better to do.

"Oh, are you too busy? Some prior engagement holding you back?" Charles rose from the table and began to pace the floor. Henry rolled his eyes, swallowing the drink in his mouth.

It had been often said that when Henry sat still on a night such as this, that he looked remarkably similar to a painting. His dark, smooth hair hung

Praise for *EMERALD GREEN*

"I loved this book! ...one of the best romance novels I have read in a while"

*—Nerd Girl*

"...this one definitely hit the spot. I can't wait for the next book...!"

*—Kylie's Fiction Addiction*

"This book was all kinds of amazing. I loved every word of it. Sooo good!"

*—Amazon Reviewer*

"I can't wait to get my hands on the next book. I need more!!"

*—Amazon Reviewer*

"This book is awesome! I can't wait to read what happens in the next story."

*—Amazon Reviewer*

"This author is incredibly talented... This was an amazing five star read! This book was SO good! I can't wait to see what happens next in the series!!"

*—Amazon Reviewer*

down, nearly touching the length of his neck, to better frame his face. He had a strong jawline, high cheekbones, and altogether a face which looked as though it had been sculpted by an artist instead of being the natural result of procreation. A painting he was, indeed.

"I just think it will be a waste of time, that's all." Henry studied the playing cards spread out on the table before him. What was first intended to be a game of poker, now seemed more akin to solitaire, as it was Henry, sitting alone with the ace of spades, while Charles spoke just to hear himself talk.

"A waste of time?" Charles shot back. "What has ever been so important to keep you in this place every minute of every day? New York will be right here when you return, just as you left it." He filled another glass of wine, sipping at it cheerfully, as he surveyed the fine globe sitting on the table nearest the window.

"And if there is no me to return?" Henry relaxed into his chair, pressing his back against its soft cushioning. Eyeing his friend very carefully, Henry held a strong gaze, though the older companion, more equipped with skills of persuasion, had won from the very start.

Charles placed his free hand on the globe, a golden ring shining on his shortest finger. "Men all over this world have given their lives dying," he spun the globe around, as he went on, "not afraid to sacrifice for the cause." Charles looked out the window into the night. "And all of their lives have meant something, because they were noble enough to be remembered."

"And they're all dead now too," Henry retorted.

Charles turned away from the window, facing Henry with a look of disappointment. The globe continued to spin behind him in the background. "Do you mock the men whose blood was shed just so people like you could have a chance?" His face had turned red, matching the curly tendrils of his hair, which shared the same hue.

"No, sir," Henry replied, remembering his place by the older fellow.

"Then don't speak of such people as if you never knew them," Charles commanded.

"But I *didn't* know them," Henry grew bold enough to say. "Besides, this is no war you're speaking of. You just want to go abroad." Henry collected the cards on the table and shuffled them into one large deck.

"The men who embark on this voyage will be remembered in history, for all time."

"I don't believe it," Henry interrupted with a sly smile. "The New World has already been discovered. Whatever minuscule territories you collect from the sea are of no importance. It is land, vast undivided land. That is what matters now." Henry stood, finishing the last bit of wine from his glass. "Now, if you'll excuse me, we'll call it an evening."

Charles nodded towards him and set his wine glass down on the table. "Fine then. Remember, I won't be able to go fishing with you for some time, nor hunting neither." He approached Henry, taking his hand to shake when it was offered to him. "If you should change your mind," Charles said on his way towards the door.

"I won't." Henry was firm, growing aggravated with the current degree of tension between the two friends.

"I must tell you, dear Henry, I fear that you are making a mistake."

"No," Henry said, "you are."

With an apathetic glance, Henry nodded at Charles, asking for his departure. Charles shrugged, placing a top hat over his head before stepping through the door. He walked the length of the vast floor that led him to the front entrance. There, he stepped across the threshold and into the warm night, leaving Henry at the family estate to think for himself.

* * *

The next morning, Henry woke to find his mother bombarding him with inquiries about his present disposition. "Abigail Ellis is a fine girl. Perhaps you should call on her today." She spoke like a mother bird feeding her biddies, wanting the words in her mouth to suddenly appear in his.

"No, Mother." Henry only looked at the plate before him, his main focus to eat the meal at hand.

"Oh, what about Emmaline Winters? She was

quite lovely when I saw her last." Mrs. Rochester always behaved in such a manner when Henry's father was out of town on business, as he was presently.

"No, Mother," he repeated, inhaling his tea with one resounding gulp.

"Henry," Mrs. Rochester scolded, "I do not know what is the matter with you. Are none of the ladies to please you in New York? What's wrong with Emmaline?"

"She is too pretty," he quickly rebutted, without even meeting her eyes.

"And Abigail?"

"Too plain." He smirked at her, the light golden color of his eyes brightening at the small victory.

Mrs. Rochester threw her cloth napkin down, covering her plate of uneaten food. "Why you take pleasure in defying me, I will never know. My only son!" She threw her hands in the air, lifting her face to the ceiling in disgust. "If only I'd had another."

Henry smiled at his mother without showing any teeth, for although their family fortune was large, indeed, it was up to the sole discretion of his father as to how it should be allocated. And since Mr. Rochester had been in no hurry to enter into holy matrimony when he was a young man, he saw no need in pushing Henry towards a woman he did not love, nor wish to hear speak.

"Find me a lady who will disagree, and I'll call

on her every day." Henry rose from the table, acknowledging Mrs. Rochester. "Mother." He nodded, then headed upstairs to his room.

"Uh," she whined to the servants, fussing at them about matters which were of no importance to Henry.

Upstairs, he looked through the long, sweeping view of the town offered by his bedroom window. Down below, he saw Charles and the others headed for the docks. His eyes followed them with curiosity, as he had imagined them to have left hours ago. He had never anticipated the opportunity to still be alive.

When he heard his mother shouting at him from downstairs, Henry left his bedroom just for the sake of his own amusement. But Henry froze when he reached the banister at the top of the staircase, for both Abigail and Emmaline were standing in the doorway. His eyes widened in terror, as his mother made playful, nice conversation with the girls.

Abigail was sixteen, with soft, white blonde curls, powder blue eyes, and a fine complexion, though her wit could be equated to that of a frog's. He had yet to have a single conversation with the girl, without her snorting at his remarks, even when they were not funny. Emmaline, on the other hand, was two years older, with a much lovelier face and figure. Her features were dark where Abigail's were light, as Emmaline's hair and eyes were a shade of dark brown. With the exception of their ivory toned skin, the two girls looked nothing alike, and even though Emmaline was the fairer of the two, she was much too agreeable to be really so.

Instead of laughing at every word Henry said, Emmaline agreed with it wholly, so that an entire conversation would pass without her uttering a single thought of her own, other than, "You are so right. I agree with you immensely." She often interchanged the two phrases, every now and then adding, "I never thought of it that way before," to soften the monotony. It rarely helped.

"Oh, Henry." Mrs. Rochester smiled when she saw his figure nearing the staircase. "Come down, you have visitors." She winked at Abigail, causing the girl to snort with giggling laughter.

"Give me just a moment, Mother." Henry quickly turned on his heel and scurried into his bedroom. He slammed the door behind him, startling his mother when he did so.

"Come now, girls." Mrs. Rochester grinned, directing the ladies into one of the sitting rooms. "Let us have tea." She eyed Henry's bedroom door, suspicious of what he could be up to in there.

In his room, Henry had begun hurriedly packing a trunk with clothing and toiletries. With his father away on business and his younger sister, Louisa, traveling abroad, Henry knew that there was no way he could endure staying with his mother alone. She was determined to have him married off by the season's end, but Henry would have nothing of it.

Checking the window, Henry noticed that the party of men bound to go island hunting was preparing to depart. Quickly sliding into his overcoat, Henry grabbed the well-packed trunk and barreled down the staircase. Once at the front door, he grabbed his hat and placed it over his head.

"My Henry, good God!" Mrs. Rochester shouted from the bordering room where she was seated with Abigail and Emmaline, having tea. "Where are you going?"

"With Charlie, we're headed out across the Atlantic." Henry felt the chains unbinding as he said the words.

"With that party of men? That's dangerous to be out there at sea so long. Something could happen to you," she added, just to be melodramatic. "What if I never see you again?"

Henry looked at the two girls, who were in such a state of shock, that for the first time in his presence, Abigail was incapable of snorting. Then, turning to his mother, Henry quipped, "So be it." With a devilish smile on his face, he offered a modest bow. "Good morning."

And so he left the women crying over their tea as he raced out into the street, arriving at the vessel just in time. "Charlie!" he yelled out, noticing his good friend loading from the docks.

"Henry!" Charles was exceedingly glad that his

young friend had arrived. "So, you decided to join the party after all?" The two hugged, slapping each other on the back.

"I'm afraid so." Henry smiled, glad to be so well-received.

"Hey, Worthing!" Charles yelled across the way at the gray-haired man who had orchestrated the whole affair and was overseeing the entire party for the duration of the voyage. "Look who decided to show up." Charles grinned, wrapping his arm around Henry's shoulder.

"Glad you finally decided to join us, Henry," Worthing spoke. "I know this one will be more content with you around." He nodded towards Charles.

"Thank you, sir." Henry let go of his luggage as Charles took it from him, moving it below deck where he was storing his own belongings. "How long can I expect to be gone on this grand adventure?" Henry looked out at the blue sea and breathed in her fresh, salty air.

"One year," was Worthing's cold reply, while he shuffled past Henry, giving orders to remove the anchors and untie the ropes.

Suddenly, it dawned on Henry that he may very well never see New York again. He had not anticipated the journey to last so long. Looking out from the harbor, Henry began to wonder if he had made a terrible mistake, all out of rash desperation and longing. He had not even been able to tell his father goodbye, nor his sister, Louisa, for that matter. Swallowing his fear, Henry turned his back on the harbor and looked out on the shining waters instead. He could only hope that this voyage would not end as others he had heard of in the past had – with a watery grave.

## Chapter 2

O nce departed, the men felt triumphant, for they had succeeded in leaving the rest of the world behind. Most of the party consisted of married men, already with several children. But Charles and Henry were of the few who remained unwed. Nevertheless, all the men got on remarkably well with one another, sharing old stories over whiskey and gin. The ship's esteemed captain even took to the relaxed atmosphere, once they had been at sea for nearly a week.

Henry and Charles stayed below deck, sleeping on cots that had been arranged like bunk beds. Every man kept his belongings on a separate shelf, though most were storing common goods in the large closet down below.

And so, the voyage continued, for one month and then two. Before they knew it, the spring season had passed them by, as the weather began to accommodate the spirit of summer.

"Hey, Charlie." Henry lay on his cot, while

Charles rested on the one up above.

"Yes, Henry." Charles let his arm dangle over the thin mattress. Henry noticed the gold ring on Charles's finger, the item clearly identifying the speaker.

"We've been gone nearly three months now, and yet I feel as though it's been a year." Henry let out a deep breath.

"You wish you hadn't come?" Charles leaned over the edge for a moment, so that Henry could see his face. "Is that what you're saying?"

"No." Henry shook his head, running a palm over the lines of his face that were now marked with worry.

Charles lay back, resting his head on the pillow beneath him. "Then what is it, young friend?"

Henry rolled to his side, placing a palm beneath the side of his face. "I thought we'd come for adventure, discovery. We haven't seen a speck of land since we left New York. Have we come all this way for nothing?"

"You're just tired," Charles mused, rolling over to face the wall. "Get some sleep, Henry. We'll be closer by morning." He grew quiet, soon snoring loudly enough for the fish to hear. Henry shrugged, turning over to change the position of his body, as he could not seem to get comfortable. Eventually, exhaustion took him, and he fell into a deep sleep.

\* \* \*

Henry woke in an abrupt manner, for

someone was shaking him out of his relaxed state. Upon opening his eyes, Henry found one of the crewmen standing before him. He was wet and trembling, causing Henry to shout at him in alarm.

"Good God sir, what's the matter?"

"We're in the middle of a storm. It's getting stronger and I don't know if she can take it." The crewman studied the wooden boarding of the room below deck.

"Who?" Henry placed his arm on the man's shoulder.

"The ship!" He stormed off, alerting other passengers as Henry woke Charles.

"We best join the rest on deck." Charles climbed down from the top bunk, stepping into his shoes. "I do believe you'll get your adventure after all." He left Henry to himself, as he disappeared to offer his help upstairs.

"You're the one who wanted adventure." Henry sat down on the bed for a moment, hearing the wailing cries of the ocean storm. As the tumbling waves caused the ship to jostle, Henry had trouble getting his shoes on and crashed into the opposite wall.

Henry and Charles soon made it above deck, the former's eyes widening in terror as magnificent waves came crashing down upon the ship. Water had overtaken the vessel, subtly drowning the wooden exterior. Boards split and glass shattered, causing a panic to ripple across all on board.

The older men grabbed buckets and pales of

all different shapes and sizes, trying their best to give the unwanted water back to its salty mother. However, as the storm wore on, new leaks sprang up from the bottom of the ship, turning their daydream voyage into a deadly nightmare.

"Come now, quick," Charles declared, grabbing Henry by the collar. He untied one of the wooden lifeboats, then used the ropes to slowly lower it down over the other side. Charles climbed over and sat in the boat, preparing the paddles, though his small vessel nearly flipped in the process. "Come, Henry," Charles yelled up at him, while Henry stood looking out at the violent waters.

"Look at these people!" Henry shouted back. "We can't just leave them!"

"You stupid boy," Charles barked, rowing away in the storm. Henry watched him struggle against the current, as a lightning bolt struck in the near distance, soon growing closer to the ship.

Quite a few men had already been tossed overboard, and when the captain went, there wasn't much hope left for the rest of them. Henry could hear their wailing screams in the night, as each was taken by the unrelenting ocean storm. In no time at all, the ship's foundation began to split in half, causing it to sink beneath rough waters.

Henry slid against the slippery deck floor, crashing into the railing before he was thrown overboard. He came down upon the water with much force, causing his arms and legs to flail outward. Kicking for the surface, Henry barely kept his head above water, still fighting against the current. He swam away from the collapsing ship, even as the crushing waves beat against his body with tremendous strength.

In a matter of moments, nearly all of the ship was submerged beneath the water, as several men clung to its wooden remains for dear life. The small lifeboat Charles had taken to escape in had now been reduced to a mere paddle.

"Charlie!" Henry drifted, searching for his friend. He was giving out with exhaustion, until a pale body with fiery orange hair floated his way. "Charlie!" Henry swam towards him, turning the body around so he could see its face. "Oh good God," he moaned, looking down at the corpse of his best friend. "Oh no, no Charlie," he cried out, hugging Charles's lifeless flesh to him. "No." He let go and watched Charlie slowly drift away.

Just as suddenly as the storm had begun, the tide grew quiet again, and the restless night subsided. Soon, Henry saw the sun, and began counting the twenty-five bodies that were floating on the surface of the sea. With what strength he had left, Henry swam. He swam the farthest distance that he could away from the wreckage and bodies. And even as they became tiny specks in the distance, Henry soon found that his overall scenery had not changed at all, for he was still floating in the middle of the ocean on a wooden plank from the ship.

Henry did not know the length of time which passed after that. It may have been days, weeks. Yet, Henry would do no more than silently drift in the water, the image of Charles's cold, white face constantly reappearing in his mind. He watched the sun rise and set, felt hunger and thirst, and wondered how it was that he, the youngest of them all, the last one to board the ship, had been the only one to survive.

Then, one day, when the sun was preparing to center itself in the sky, Henry felt still, peaceful somehow, as if the water had stopped moving him. Henry slowly opened his eyes to find himself lying on his stomach, his hands pressed into the sandy shore beneath him. He moved his fingers, and as they dug into the damp ground, his face lifted. Holding that small clump of wet sand in the air caused Henry to look forward, where he discovered a tropical island in the midst of the sea.

In astonishment, Henry staggered to his feet, not minding the waves that still flowed against the back of his knees. Pushing the hair from his face, Henry crawled towards the lush paradise, finding it hard to move on such weak muscles. His mouth hung open, so full of hunger and thirst that he yelped in delight once he discovered a table of food, covered with exotic fruits, leafy vegetables, and fine grains.

There was a small wooden shack, just bordering the area where Henry ate like a mad man, shoving as much sustenance as he could into his mouth at once. He closed his eyes, taking a thankful breath, as he had never felt so grateful for food in his entire life.

Except for the small shack and table where Henry had found the food, the rest of the land remained a tropical beach. From what Henry had noticed so far, a forest began where the sand ended, and if he were to walk deeper, he might find running water.

Taking one last piece of fruit, Henry stepped towards the shack, whose door frame was covered only by a transparent sheet of white fabric. He moved closer, for behind the cloth he saw a young woman sleeping, her body outstretched on a small rectangular section of bedding against the wall.

He took another step, only to make out the image of her face, framed in a glossy mane of raven black hair. However, with that step, a deep, haunting growl sounded from the border of the jungle. Just as quickly as Henry had shifted his eyes to observe the noise, a black panther, long and sleek, emerged from the woods. Fearless, the creature soared through the air and pounced on top of Henry. Before he could understand what was happening, the snarling black cat held an enormous paw over him, and then swiped its claws across his chest.

Henry wailed in panic and terror, using his arms to push the cat off him, as it pinned him to the ground by the flat of his back. The creature clawed at Henry's stomach in protest, while the young man did the best he could to protect his face.

During the struggle, Henry had never felt so near the bottom of the food chain in all his life. He was paralyzed with fear as the great cat hovered over his body, with such a close distance that no human ever lived to talk about. But what terrified Henry the most, above the shiny, slimy white fangs, were the panther's piercing green eyes, so alive with the greenery of the forest, that they could have been cut from the leaves of a vine for all he knew. They were so perfectly round and rigid, that they nearly looked like stones, though not the exact color of emerald. And yet it was these cat's eyes, those jungle eyes, which made his heart stop.

"Jade," a soft, transcendent voice called from above. The cat retreated immediately, slowly walking away from Henry.

Sunlight shone on Henry's face as he lay flat, still on the ground. He lowered his eyes, horrified by the blood stains on his white ocean-soaked shirt. But then, the face of a lovely woman stood before the sun, blocking out its light. Henry looked up at her, taking in the long, silky black hair; golden, sun-kissed skin; and green eyes – so much like the jungle he had just discovered.

She narrowed her eyes, looking over Henry's body as he felt her pulling him into a trance, mesmerizing him with her beauty. Then, for he had not seen it coming, Henry felt a tremendous pain enter the side of his head. All of a sudden, he noticed an object in her hand that she had just bludgeoned him with. But before the blue sky faded to black, the last thing Henry remembered was the natural hue of her glistening green jungle eyes.

## Chapter 3

**H**enry woke to find himself stretched out on a cot, with strips of cloth wrapped around his midsection. He lifted his elbows to prop himself up, but as he did so, the act of leaning his head forward reaffirmed the terrible discomfort there. "Ah," he groaned, gritting his teeth together. At the same time, Henry had a tremendous headache, which throbbed with the tenacity of a thousand raging bulls.

Henry sat up in the small space where he had been kept and swung his legs over the edge of the cot, no matter the pain in his abdomen. With a hand to his throbbing head, Henry glanced about the room. There was another cot, identical to his, resting against the opposite wall. A table was centered in the right half of the room, with a bureau against the wall, not so distantly placed from the other cot.

On the table sat flowers and plants of different sorts, as well as several sheets of what appeared to be some sort of fabric, intended for clothing perhaps. Henry rose and upon approaching the table, was so overcome with thirst, that he thought he might faint.

There was a transparent, filmy layer of fabric that hung over the open doorway, and when a young woman swept through the entrance, Henry was so startled that he nearly knocked the table over. Remembering what she had done to him, Henry gripped the edge of the table with his hands.

"You stay back!" he yelled, frightened by the profound fearlessness in her eyes.

She wore a fitted white dress, which fell just above the knee, whose sleeves came to her elbows. The soft, light material clung to her feminine shape in all the right places, especially where it formed a circular cut just above her breast. Henry had never seen such a fashion before, but he was not one to judge a woman's clothing. Her tan skin deeply contrasted with the white fabric, just as her jet-black hair contrasted with her green eyes. With a large pitcher in her hands, she took a step forward and approached him.

"Stop, or I'll-" Henry reached behind him, scrambling to find something of use on the table.

"You'll what?" she scoffed, offering the pitcher to him. "It's just water."

Henry glanced at the pitcher, then looked her over. In all his life, he had never seen so much skin of a woman before, nor had he found anything so beautiful.

"Fine," she hissed, setting the pitcher down on the table, as Henry moved away. "I frighten you?" She wondered at the statement, finding the thought ridiculous as he was both taller and male.

"You attacked me," he accused, as if there was no other way about the situation.

"Well, actually, Jade was the one who did the attacking," she corrected, raising a pair of jet-black eyebrows.

Henry leaned on the table, placing his palm down to keep his balance. "After your creature attacked me, you hit me over the head with a rock!"

It took a mere second for her to fight back.

"You stole my food," she countered, folding her arms across her chest. "I'm a young woman, living here alone, and here comes a strange man that I have never seen in all my life. How did you expect me to react?" Taking a few steps back, she sat down on Henry's cot and turned her head towards the table outside, where he had ravenously consumed her food earlier.

"Well, I'm sorry." Henry felt the need to apologize, the gentleman in him coming out. "I was traveling with a group of men, and we were overtaken by a storm. The ship was destroyed, and I am the only one who survived. Somehow, I washed ashore here." He winced at the pain in his head, placing a palm there.

The young woman listened to Henry as he

spoke, then simply nodded. "All right then," she declared, gliding towards the doorway. "Those should be changed soon." She pointed at the bandages tied nicely around his abdomen. "To prevent infection, of course. It sounds like you've had a rough journey. I'll be back to check on you later. For now, you should get some rest." She pulled the transparent layer of fabric back as it rippled in the windy passage of the doorway.

"Wait," Henry called after her, as she leaned back into the room. "What's your name?"

"Elaine." She grinned without showing any teeth.

"I'm Henry," he added, feeling modest in his shirtless state, yet too exhausted to act it.

"It's nice to meet you, Henry," she muttered, her voice enveloping the tone of a serious nature. "Get some rest."

Henry watched her silhouette as she walked away.

* * *

By the time Henry woke, the sky had turned pitch black, with a full moon rising in the night sky up above. He rose from the cot and pressed his hand over the new bandages. Elaine had replaced them when he was nearly unconscious, drifting in and out of sleepless states. Now, Henry was overcome with a state of hunger, far beyond the degree of pain he felt across his abdomen. The new bandages had not soaked through, so Henry slid his arms through the white button-down shirt that had been laying out to dry.

Outside the shack, Elaine tended a large fire, the dancing flames casting a glow about her face. Henry moved through the filmy white sheet draped over the doorway and watched Elaine carefully, as he sat down across from her. She cautiously scrutinized him around the fire, her green eyes vibrant and alive, though the evening had grown sleepy, with the lofty moon and gently-crashing waves down below.

"Here." Elaine rose from the sandy ground and walked over to Henry. "Take it." She shoved a bowl full of fish in his direction, her impatient temper showing.

"Thank you." He looked up at her while taking the food, careful not to let his hand touch hers. Henry placed a palm against his rib cage, gritting his teeth together as he knelt down in the sand. Extending his legs outward, Henry continued to wince in pain, eventually finding a position that was bearable enough to tolerate.

Elaine sat back down at the fire, opposite Henry, pulling her legs inward as she pressed her heels into the cool sand. She looked towards the ocean, as if his presence were of no importance to her, as if he were merely a placeholder that she had no way of replacing.

Henry took a piece of fish out of the bowl, and it still felt warm to the touch. He assumed that Elaine must have cooked it over the fire earlier. As her eyes moved towards the vast sea and its blue, crushing waves, Henry placed the fish in his mouth, not paying a terrible amount of attention to the flavor. Then, after several moments of prolonged silence, he set the bowl aside, with a few pieces remaining, and stole glances at Elaine from across the fire.

"So." Henry ran a hand through his dark locks. "How did you come to be here?"

Elaine looked up at him, though only for an instant, before her eyes fell to the ground, as if the weight of speaking was pulling them downward. Henry tried to bring her eyes back to his, but it was to no avail, as she began to form prints in the dirt with her hands.

"How long have you been here?" Henry's lips remained apart, even when he finished speaking. He smiled, to be polite, secretly hoping to meet her eyes.

Elaine pulled her knees into her body, wrapping her arms around them by the bend in her elbows. She looked towards the left, far across the beach, at some distant significance that Henry was unaware of. Growing tired of her mute responses, Henry lurched forward, despite the pain in his chest and abdomen, nearly coming too close to the flames.

In that moment, Elaine opened her glistening green eyes for him, affirming his very fear. She met his warm, unyielding gaze and held her jaw taut, as if she were ready to attack. "Longer than you can imagine." She let the words go without emotion, though so much time had needed to pass for her to be able to say them. Her jawline stayed firm as she studied him, daring him to ask her to go on.

Returning her gaze, Henry became paralyzed with fear, his throat suddenly growing dry as he gulped down a breath of fresh air. Behind Elaine, along the nearest edge of forest, the black panther came out into the night, slowly prowling, as she made her way to the fire.

"Why have you grown so quiet?" Elaine wondered, suddenly disappointed that it had been so easy a task to silence him. "What is it? What are you staring at?" She looked over her shoulder to find the long, sleek black cat stalking towards them in the night. "Oh," she chuckled, glancing at Henry with a playful smirk. He sat with his hands firmly pressed into the ground, his blood boiling as the rate of his heart increased. Henry's eyes remained wide with fear, as he began to sweat along the plane of his forehead, despite the evening breeze. "Come, Jade." Elaine motioned with her hand.

Henry was confused and disgruntled by the genuinely pleasant smile on her face. She couldn't actually be friendly with this beast. Could she?

The cat drew close to Elaine, lying down on the sand beside her as she rubbed a careful hand along the cat's head, eventually scratching the place just beneath its chin and around its neck. Henry watched on in horror, his heart nearly beating out of his chest, as the creature began to purr, making a noise much deeper and more terrifying than any house cat he had ever heard. As the panther relaxed, her jaws opened wide, revealing a sharp set of white fangs, just as lethal-looking as he had remembered them up close.

Growing more comfortable, the cat laid her long legs out across Elaine's bare-skinned legs, and before too long, a black flesh-tearing paw was resting on the top of Elaine's thigh. She continued to massage the big cat, stroking her shoulders and chest, her hands softly rubbing the large feline ears. When her gaze finally returned to Henry, who was so near a deathly shade of white that he looked ill, her brow furrowed in concern.

"How can you sit there so calmly?" Henry spoke when he had mustered up enough courage to breathe in front of the panther.

"She's not going to hurt me." Elaine shook her head, briefly glancing down at the very large cat in her lap.

"But she could." Henry stared at her black fur paws and the deadly claws attached to them, quickly shifting his gaze to the slimy fangs not far from Elaine's face. "Doesn't it frighten you?" He glanced down in front of the fire and spotted the bowl with the remaining pieces of fish. Just as Henry was reaching for it, in an attempt to make peace with his animal enemy, Elaine stopped him.

"Don't," she demanded, causing his hand to freeze in mid-air, just over the fish. "I don't feed her." Elaine held his gaze, glowering until he pulled his hand back into his lap.

"Why?" Henry wasn't sure if he was more afraid of her or the predator in her lap.

"She shouldn't depend on me." Elaine slowly brushed her fingers against the back of the cat's neck.

"Then what do you call this?" Henry did not expect an answer, though longed for one just the same.

"We're in the wild, Henry. She can fend for herself." Elaine kept her eyes on him, though her palms rested against the panther's fur coat.

"How do I know she won't attack me again?" Henry leaned on the side of his elbow, yet still did not feel completely secure within the panther's presence.

"She knows you're not here to hurt me. She can sense it." Elaine gazed down at the panther, watching her breathing grow slow and steady. "It's her animal instinct."

"And before?"

"You were just a stranger taking my food." Elaine smiled, glad that she had been the one to settle the disagreement.

"Why does she let you get so close and touch her like that?" Henry pointed at the cat, who gazed over at him with a pair of glazed-over eyes.

"You mean, why does she get so close to me?" Elaine patted the cat's smooth, silky fur. "I've had her since she was a cub. I'm the only mother she's ever known."

Henry watched the uncanny way that the big cat looked up into Elaine's eyes – it was unreal. But it did remind him of the way a mother and child might act towards one another, human or not.

"There's something between the two of you. It's so strange, so unnatural. Against mother nature, against what it means to be human." Henry stared at the two of them, woman and panther, yet he could not put his finger on it. How was it possible that the forces of nature, the innate drive to kill, the inborn instinct to survive, had not been enough to separate them?

"It's simple." Elaine's eyes beamed across the fire, holding his gaze. "If I were an animal, I'd be her. And if she were human, she'd be me."

Henry sat back in disbelief, noticing what had been so obvious all along. Elaine's long, silky black hair hung down to the length of her waist, the look of it akin to the cat's deep, black fur coat. Elaine gleamed at him through a pair of wild, exotic green jungle eyes, while the cat's bore a resemblance much of the same. They were two emblems of nature, trapped in the surroundings of their own destiny. Yet somehow, they were two pieces of the same spirit. Despite the boundaries of nature and time, they were here together, in this same place. The same human. The same animal. The same soul.

"She's beautiful," Henry stated, as if his words

were no matter of opinion.

"I always said she was a pretty cat." Elaine watched over her, then caught Henry's eye, and from the solemn look on his face, could decipher his meaning. "Thank you." She felt a tinge of red in her cheeks, hoping that he would not be able to see for the firelight.

"Did you find her?" Henry studied the way Elaine's hands moved over the cat's body, and for a moment, wanted to be that very cat.

"Something like that." She was not one for elaborating, as Henry was beginning to discover.

"I take it you're never going to give me the full story, are you?" Henry sat up, his elbows weak from resting on them for too long.

"About what?" She coyly smirked, knowing she had lost no amount of intrigue.

"How you came to be here, how long you've been here, how long you've been petting this cat." Henry chuckled at the last, not denying the fact that her defiance was something he admired most about her. Elaine bit her lip, hiding the coquettish grin on her face. "So bits and pieces then, eh?"

Elaine nodded, her gaze shifting as she watched him rise to his feet. "Bits and pieces."

With that, Henry trudged towards the shelter, moving his way through the cloth-covered doorway. Easing himself onto the mattress, Henry placed his palm across his abdomen, closing his eyes as he prepared to fall asleep. But just before drifting off completely, he could not help but remember the sweet, motherly radiance that had glowed from Elaine's youthful skin before the fire.

## Chapter 4

When Henry woke the next morning, he was more than pleased to see the sun. Charles had been on his mind lately, filling his nightmares with terror and guilt. Try as he might, Henry could not overcome the fact that he was the only one left. He felt as though it were somehow his fault, that in order for him to live, all of the others had been forced to die.

Ruffling a hand through his messy locks, Henry sat up in the cot, clutching his abdomen once he felt a steady balance come over him. The pieces of fabric around his midsection had changed color due to his bodily fluids leaking out. He used his finger and thumb to pull back one of the bandages, exposing a crusty cut that had not ceased to ooze. Wincing in pain, Henry stepped onto the floor and walked through the filmy fabric-covered entryway.

The sun was nearing the center of the sky as Henry shielded his eyes from the burning light.

He walked past the darkened patch of sand, where Elaine had made a fire the night before. Looking out across the shore, Henry searched for the girl, but could not seem to make her image out anywhere. There was no food on the table, as there had been before, and Henry was of too ignorant a mind and damaged a body to hope to fend for himself.

Henry stood quietly for a moment, watching the breeze drift through the tropical paradise, until he heard a noise coming from the bordering stretch of forest. He listened again, more intently this time, noting that the sound was most certainly female. Turning towards the woods, Henry paused, looking back to make sure no one was watching him and no cat was hunting him. Then, ever so carefully, Henry took a stealthy step forward and entered the jungle.

Looking up, Henry observed the tops of the highest trees, decorated with rich green foliage. Colorful birds moved about the trees, flying from and towards one another. Exotic insects and infinitesimal creatures of the strangest variety danced along the bark of each passing tree. Henry smiled, gazing about the vast supply of natural beauty. He breathed in the smell of sweet, wonderful, heavenly scents, as he passed varying breeds of flora and fauna along the way. With every sight he took in, Henry knew that, if not for his last-minute decision to leave New York, he would have lived his whole life without ever experiencing any of this.

At the sound of bubbling laughter, Henry continued on his journey through the forest. As he moved closer to the sound, he began to hear an overpowering gust of rushing water. Anxious to see with his eyes what his ears were already able to hear, Henry quickened his pace, nearly tripping over tree roots that ran as veins along the forest floor, until the jungle blended into an open, light area containing a waterfall and the lagoon it fed down below.

Henry stopped, watching a spectrum of light form in the sky as the sunshine hit the falling water at a certain angle. He leaned on a nearby tree, gazing out at the beautiful new world surrounding him. The most genuine smile of pure joy spread across the lower half of his face, creating a new expression altogether. Never before had Henry witnessed land that made him feel as though his whole being, body and soul, had just been cleansed in the deepest waters of the earth, providing him with the feeling that he could start anew, for he was new, and in a new world.

Just as Henry was reveling in his moment of clarity, a new addition to the scenery before him fell into view. He took a step back to disguise himself, as Elaine swam under the waterfall, surfacing in the clear blue pool. Her long black hair lay over her bare back, damp and glistening in the sunlight. As she floated in the water, the naked skin above her breast glowed beneath the sunny, tropical breeze. Though he could not see her naked body through the water, her bare back and shoulders were enough for him to understand that he had intruded upon her daily bathing ritual. Upon closer observation, he spotted the black panther resting on one of the larger boulder-like rocks that comprised a small section of land scattered with long, flat structures made of stone. The cat lay in a very relaxed manner, on her stomach with her left front leg dangling over the rock in a careless fashion.

Henry turned away quickly, retreating the way he came. Guilt crept into the pit of his stomach, for he knew that he had seen something that he wasn't supposed to have seen. Rushing back to the shack, Henry placed his hands on his knees to catch his breath. He moved through the door frame and lay back down on the cot. The feeling in his stomach spread, slowly progressing into a delightful, tingling sensation. Henry wondered at the feeling, for he had never had one like it before. It was an ache in his hands and a yearning in his bones. He rose from the cot, pacing the floor, and even jumped in place until the strange, violent feeling had subsided.

A few moments later, Elaine swept through the doorway, startling Henry, who was still circling the room with his hands on his hips, though in a slower fashion. She was wearing a different dress than the one he had seen her in before. It was shorter in length and had no sleeves, but two thin straps over her shoulders that connected the front part of the dress with the back. The color of the dress resembled the white one, although it was a light, washed-out shade of green. It almost looked as though she had drowned the fabric in the waters of the sea, which had made sure to leave a lasting impression.

Her hair was still wet, though not dripping, and as she moved past him to place the clothing she had slept in the night before away, his breathing pattern increased.

"Henry?" She spoke to him with her back turned. When he did not answer, she questioned him further. "Henry, are you all right?"

He moved to the cot, sitting down to rest his head in his hands. "Yes," he uttered, though the sound was muffled. "I'm fine," he declared, unable to look at her.

"Are you sure?" Elaine walked towards him, looking over his tragic state. She didn't believe him.

"Yes," he repeated, much louder this time.

"How long have you been awake?" She studied his appearance with wonder, searching for his face beneath the pair of hands that covered it.

"Not long." Henry forced the words out in a rush, quickly tearing his hands away from his face. Elaine wore a look of concern, for she could not fathom why his eyes would not meet hers.

"Let me take a look." She opened the remaining part of his shirt that had been left buttoned. Henry gazed up at her, seeing the golden hue of her skin and smelling the fresh, floral scent of her raven-colored locks. "Oh my." Elaine peeled a section of the bandages back enough to expose his abdomen. "Henry." She met his eyes, before quickly returning her focus to the wounds on his body.

"Is there something wrong?" Henry studied Elaine's face, more content with her reaction than the one he had bestowed earlier

"Well," she stalled, not sure how to put it. "Most of these cuts are oozing, and some of them are still bleeding." Henry winced as she removed the rest of the bandages, though he did not express a desire to keep her from doing so. "Sorry." She felt guilty for Henry's injuries, since Jade had been the one to cause them.

Henry made no remark at her apology. He was still trying to maintain a steady heart rate, as her soft fingertips pressed against his skin.

"It just needs to be cleaned," Elaine assured him. Helping him outside, she instructed him to rest at the base of one of the palm trees. So, Henry sat down in the sand, leaning his head back beneath the shade. He closed his eyes, relaxing for a moment, until she returned with a clean cloth and fresh water.

Elaine dipped the cloth in the water, then began to wipe away the bloody, liquid substance that had formed around the wounds. "Ah," Henry winced in pain, firmly grabbing Elaine by the wrist to make her stop. "Not so rough." He stared into her eyes with a knowing look.

Elaine returned the cloth to the water again, and then pressed the damp material to Henry's skin, more gently this time. They stole glances at each other every so often, until Elaine had finished. She left him alone, though only for a moment, then returned with a pasty green substance in a small bowl, similar in style to the kind they had eaten out of the night before.

Without asking, Elaine dipped two fingers in the paste, moving closer to place it on his wounds. Henry held his hand out in protest before she could touch his skin. "What is this?" He looked down, resistant at first, as he sent a questioning look her way.

"It will help your wounds heal quicker. I've put it on all sorts of cuts and scrapes." She rested on her knees, sinking deeper into the sand while he contemplated her strange concoction.

"What is it made out of?" Henry leaned down to smell the substance in the bowl.

"Just leaves and some fruit." She offered the remedy to him, willing to let him take as much as he wanted.

"All right," he finally succumbed, balancing the bowl in his palm.

"It's probably best if I do it," she insisted, taking the bowl back from him. "It can get messy if you don't know what you are doing." Focusing on Henry's stomach, she rubbed the mixture between her fingers, and then began patting it onto his wounds.

To his own surprise, Henry sighed in relief as she coated the thick lines, where her panther had attacked him, with the soothing substance. Henry looked off at the ocean waves before gazing up at her, though her eyes were afar, tending to him in his injured state. "It feels cool on my skin." He smiled, his mouth widening. "What a relief."

Elaine was slow, but gentle, as she spread the paste along the areas of his skin that had been ripped open by the panther's claws. "Where did everything come from?" Henry asked all of a sudden, catching Elaine off guard.

"What do you mean?" She kept her eyes on his torso, massaging the paste in with her fingers.

"The house, the furniture, the beds, the clothing, the bowls." He gestured at the one in her hand.

"I'd hardly call it a house," she dissented, denouncing the small shelter they had to share.

"But all of it had to come from somewhere." He searched her face, a feeling of victory overpowering him when he met her eyes. "What happened, Elaine? How did you end up here?"

For a moment, she paused, not tending to his wounds. Their eyes met, and in that moment, he knew he had her. "Similar to the way you did." She rested the bowl in her lap, not minding the green residue on her fingers. "My family wanted to travel to Europe, so we boarded a cruise ship when I was twelve. Everything was going just as planned, until we got into a storm one night. The ship began to sink and we were all thrown overboard. My father found a plank of wood for us to float on, and we were the only two to survive. My mother drowned." Elaine turned to the sea, gazing at the ocean in all her majestic beauty. "My two younger sisters, and my brother," she paused, looking down at the sandy ground beneath her. "Father and I washed up onshore, and so did many of the things from the ship. That's why we have the table and the beds, the other things. And he was able to build that with what we had." She pointed to the tiny shack. "The wood's from the forest, of course. But that's how I ended up here, on this island, with my father."

Henry looked over his shoulder, searching the land surrounding him. "Well, where is he?" Henry could not understand why he wouldn't have seen him by now.

"He died when I was sixteen." Elaine returned to her work, placing the natural remedy on the remaining cuts along Henry's abdomen.

"Well, that couldn't have been very long ago. Why, you can't be more than sixteen now," Henry presumed, almost in disbelief.

"I'm twenty-one," she breathed, holding her emotions in, repressing what she wished to forget. "My father died five years ago."

Henry sat in silence, trying to come to terms with the fact that she had been living here, stranded on this island, while he had been carelessly enjoying life, spending his Saturdays in the form of lazy fishing trips with Charlie. He had failed to appreciate his home in New York, and his obnoxious, prying mother while he had the chance. For the first time, he began to feel responsible for what had happened, as if he had deserved it.

"This will feel much better soon." Elaine smiled, meeting his gaze. "I promise." She set the bowl aside, then walked a few steps to the shore to wash her hands clean. Afterwards, she came back to Henry and collected the bandages and other materials she had used, carefully avoiding his eyes.

"I'm sorry for your loss." Henry searched her face, longing to reach her, to understand her. But she quickly rose, nodding at him while her mouth tightened into a fine line. Henry looked over his shoulder and observed the outline of her body as she walked away.

\* \* \*

That night, in front of the fire, Elaine sat quietly on the ground, drawing patterns in the sand with her fingers. Henry had finished his meal in a hurry, so overcome with ravenous hunger, though he hadn't seen her eat a bite. Instead, she kept her eyes on the sand, presumably lost in her own precarious thoughts.

"I haven't seen Jade come out tonight." Henry gazed through the flames at her, glad that the silence had finally been broken.

"So you're calling her by her name now?" Elaine brushed her hands back and forth against each other, dusting the sand away. Henry said nothing, regarding her as she leaned back on her elbows, finally meeting his eyes for the first time since that afternoon. "She doesn't come out of the woods every single day, necessarily, but she's still here, and she'll be around." Elaine moved a fallen lock of hair out of her face. "In case you're worried." A smug smirk came over Elaine's face, and for some unexplained reason, he liked it.

"I had a family too, you know." Henry shrugged his shoulders, watching as the expression on Elaine's face turned to stone. "Back in New York, I had a mother and father, a young sister." Henry watched the flames dance between them, listening for the occasional popping spark. "They're all still there, I guess. They probably think I'm dead by now, like the others."

"You said New York?" Elaine sat upright, startled by what he had said.

"Yes, New York. Why do you ask?"

"Which part of New York?" She uttered the second question after he had barely finished the first.

"Manhattan." He stretched out, leaning on his elbow, with an inquisitive gaze.

"I'm from Manhattan too, near the harbor." Elaine felt exasperated as she let the words come out. She had not been the bearer of excited chatter for awhile.

"I can see the docks from my bedroom window," Henry exhaled in delight. "Why, we must have been close by all the time. What is your family's name?" Henry could hardly believe it.

"Carmichael, and yours?"

"Rochester."

They stared at each other, looks of disappointment mirroring their faces.

"That doesn't sound familiar," Henry admitted.

"Yours doesn't either." Elaine pulled her lips together, shrugging the matter off with the jerk of her shoulders.

"But New York is a growing area," Henry went on, trying to assure her of what exactly, he did not know. "Lots of people." He nodded to himself.

Elaine looked off at the distant waves, brushing the remaining sand from her palms as she stood up. "Well, Henry, good night." She turned on her heel and headed for the shack.

"I hope I didn't say anything to upset you." Henry rose from the ground, mimicking her in his method of brushing the sand from his hands.

"No, I'm very tired, Henry." Elaine walked away, then moved through the filmy white fabric draped over the doorway. Henry nodded in her direction as she left, wondering what he had done to make her leave so suddenly.

He stayed on the beach just a little while longer, before putting the fire out with a pale of ocean water. As he moved through the entrance to the shack, Henry carefully crept towards the cot he now occupied against the right wall. Lying down on the white mattress, he wondered if he had taken Elaine's spot. He remembered watching her sleep on the very cot that now belonged to him, when he had first arrived on the island. Then again, Elaine must have placed him there, because one moment he was in the sand and the next he was on the cot. He watched her now, asleep on the other identical cot that was placed against the left wall. He knew now that these must have been the beds she and her father had slept on, when he was still alive.

Henry longed to be closer to her, but withheld the desire to walk over to the cot where she slept. Elaine was so strong-willed and independent for a woman, that he wouldn't dare risk making her angry. So, he lay down on his back instead, staring up at the ceiling. He listened to the crushing tide for what seemed like hours, before finally dozing off into a restless sleep.

## Chapter 5

**E**laine was running along the shore with Jade when Henry found her the next day. The two eventually walked back to the area where a fire was made every evening, causing Henry to retreat near the entrance of the shack. Elaine knelt down in front of Jade, who similarly sank into the sand, with her paws spread out before her. Her long, sleek tail swayed back and forth, as Elaine pet her on the head and beneath the chin. Henry winced, clenching his fist, when he saw the panther extend her claws and open her mouth in a yawn, to expose those long, sharp fangs. Jade moved her head beneath Elaine's massaging touch, purring all the while.

Realizing that Henry had gone back inside, Elaine moved through the door frame tapestry, approaching him where he stood by the table. His back was to her as she moved closer. She lifted her hand to tap his shoulder, but just before touching him, Henry turned around with a defensive look on his face, as if he were questioning her motives for following him inside.

"What do you want? Are you here to let your beast attack me again?" Henry moved away from her, searching for a shirt to cover his upper body.

"No, I just thought-"

"You thought what Elaine? That I would suddenly take a liking to your pet?" He spoke over his shoulder, though never turned his head enough for her to see his whole face.

"I thought you already had," she quietly whispered to herself, folding her hands behind her back the way a scolded child might.

"Don't patronize me, Elaine." Henry faced her, buttoning his shirt while he glared in her direction.

"I'm sorry. I just wanted to show you something."

"Ah!" Henry yelled in frustration, looking down at his shirt. He had been too rough in the process of buttoning himself, for now one of the claw marks was bleeding again.

"Let me." Elaine hurried towards him, desperately wanting to help.

"No!" Henry batted her away. "You've done enough already." He tied a new strip of cloth around the wound, pressing his teeth together when he pulled too tightly.

"I don't know why you're so angry today." She crossed her arms over her chest, still reaching for something that wasn't there.

"Because that pet of yours out there did this to me!" Henry jabbed his finger towards the doorway, where the panther could be seen yawning in the sun.

With that, Elaine nodded, slowly walking back outside to Jade. Henry watched her go, hearing every nasty thing he had just said reverberate in his head. He was more angry with himself than Elaine, or even Jade, really. To release the emotion, he slammed his fist into the wall, absorbing the pain as a self-inflicted distraction.

Henry felt terribly about what he had done, so he waited inside, until Jade returned to the jungle, to catch Elaine on the beach by herself. She sat in the wet sand, letting the waves wash over her feet. The white dress covering her body enhanced the deep golden coloring of her skin. She was more beautiful than ever, and Henry hated himself for being so rude.

"I'm sorry about what I said." He stood behind her, wondering why she remained so still. "Aren't you going to say something?" Elaine stood up in one swift motion, but Henry grabbed her arm, pulling her back before she could walk away. "Look, Elaine, I'm sorry." He held her there for a moment, though she struggled to get out of his grasp, before she was finally forced to look him squarely in the eye. "Whatever it is you wanted to say to me, or show me, well, now I'm ready to listen." Henry moved a strand of hair that the breeze had suddenly blown in her face, barely touching her cheek in the process.

"Don't touch me," Elaine firmly declared, shoving his hands away from her.

Henry trailed behind her as she reached the border of the forest. "Elaine, please," he begged, touching her elbow and then quickly pulling back when he remembered what she had just said. "What is it that you wanted to show me?"

Elaine looked him over, noticing that a beard was beginning to grow on his face. His skin had slightly altered in shade, turning brown since his arrival. He was tall, dark, and handsome by most any definition of the phrase. And for reasons that even she could not understand, Elaine could not deny the fact that she liked him.

Taking a deep breath to ease her irritation, Elaine consented. "I thought it might be useful to teach you how to get food on this island. Here." She handed him a stone. "We'll start with the woods first."

Henry followed Elaine into the jungle and looked to the treetops up above. Without any warning, she knelt down behind a stretch of green shrubbery, trying to camouflage herself in the leaves. "Come here," she whispered, beckoning to Henry. He walked up beside Elaine, obliviously studying her every move. "Get down." She grabbed his shirt sleeve and pulled him to the ground beside her.

"What are we doing?" Henry whispered.

Elaine held a finger to her lips, then

encouraged him to follow her eyes. A red and yellow bird had just landed on a downward sloping branch up above. The creature cocked its head from side to side, chirping in a sing-song manner as it remained perched on the wooden limb.

"Watch me." Elaine held a round stone in her hand, carefully placing it against the elasticity of an oval-shaped band that she had fashioned with materials from the shack.

Suddenly, another bird landed on the same branch, beside the other. Elaine kept still, silently focusing on the pair of chirping creatures up above. Closing one eye completely, she positioned her thumb at the base of the strap, holding the stone in place while she aimed at the target before her. Then, confident in her skill, Elaine released the stone and watched it propel across the sky until it obliterated both birds, sending them toppling to the forest floor.

Rising from a crouched position, she retrieved her game for the day, proudly dangling them from her wrist for Henry to see. He clapped his hands together at the sight of them. "Well done." He smirked. "I don't think I've ever seen anything quite like that before."

"What?" Elaine turned on her heel, looking up at him, as if his height were no matter. "You've never seen anyone kill two birds with one stone?" A sultry, assertive smile played along the edge of her lips.

"No," Henry stated in a serious manner, as a

somber look fell over his face.

"Do you want to see something else?" Elaine swept a few fingers through her raven-black hair, a sensual expression coming over her.

"Sure." Henry pressed his lips together and followed behind as she led him through the wild, hidden parts of the forest.

Henry wanted to feel as though he could trust Elaine implicitly, but while they trampled about, moving deeper and deeper into the jungle, Henry wasn't so sure. But then a familiar sound greeted Henry as they approached the waterfall. Now he knew where he was and felt more comfortable in the present territory.

Elaine walked around the edge of the pool that was formed by the rushing waters, gazing up at the sight with a beam of admiration. "Isn't it just glorious?"

Henry stared at the falls, and then at her standing before them. "Yes," he muttered, suddenly incapable of calming the crimson-red hue of his blushing cheeks.

"Have you ever seen anything like it before, in all your life?" Elaine's eyes remained on the cool, glistening water, until she realized that Henry had not answered her.

"No." He looked down at the jungle floor, avoiding all eye contact with her. Images from the previous day, of her bathing in that very water, flooded his mind, and he could not dare meet her green eyes, for fear that she would see through the windows to his soul.

"Would you like to go for a swim?" Elaine set her hunting materials and the two birds on the ground, ready to emerge herself in the pool of water at any moment.

"No." Henry walked behind her, picking up the items she had just set down. "Let's look at something else." He walked at a rapid pace through the jungle, searching for something, anything to distract her. "Like this." Henry paused, spotting several clusters of red berries that grew along a vine on the grassy ground. "What are these?" In a rush to hurry the conversation, Henry picked a couple, aiming to pop them in his mouth, until Elaine slapped his wrist, hurriedly batting them away.

"Don't eat those, you fool! They're poison!" Elaine's heart had nearly skipped a beat at the sight of Henry putting poison in his mouth. She placed a hand over her chest, closing her eyes to take a deep breath, before Henry could see. Opening her eyes, Elaine grabbed him by the arm, pulling him after her until they reached another area surrounded by greenery and foliage.

"If you want berries," she began, closing her palm over a cluster that hung from a separate vine running along the forest floor. "These are the ones you can eat."

Noticing his vacant stare, Elaine stopped, looking over her shoulder at him as he knelt down beside her. "What?" She looked into his incredulous eyes, unsure why he had not begun to eat the berries already. "What is it?"

"These are the exact same berries. Am I mistaken?" He opened his palm out towards her and let the berries fall to the ground.

"Yes, Henry, I'm afraid you are mistaken." Elaine rose, shoving her shoulder against his, as she pushed past him, leaving the way they came. "Although, it wouldn't be the first time." She stopped in her tracks and glared at him, angry and disheartened that he had either found her to be ignorant or untruthful. Elaine could live with neither of those accusations.

"Well, what are they then?" he yelled after her, tugging at her sleeve just as she began to walk away. "You honestly believe that those berries look nothing alike?" The tone of his voice was empathetic, pleading even, as if he just wanted her to understand his point of view.

Elaine looked down at the remainder of the vine, where the last berries tapered off into the grass. "Yes," she said without making eye contact. "They are similar in appearance." There was no point in Elaine denying it. Both kinds of berries were red.

"Then how do you tell the difference between the two?" Henry stood over her with his arms carefully poised across his chest. He would not be silenced without first receiving an answer.

Elaine blew a long breath of hot air through her lips, before kneeling down to collect a handful of berries from each sort in either hand. Standing before Henry, she kept both hands tightly closed, then slowly bent her fingers back to reveal what her left palm held. "What color are these berries, Henry?"

Henry gazed at the tiny fruits in her hand, then glanced up at her eyes. "Red," he offered, thinking the question was a silly one.

"Yes, but what kind of red?" Elaine's vibrant green eyes stared into his, failing to blink as she awaited an answer.

"Dark red?" Henry placed a palm at the back of his neck, running his fingers against his hair line.

"Yes, a very deep red. These are the exact color of blood." Elaine felt the weight of Henry's eyes, contemplating her, judging her. She knew that he didn't believe her. "Now." Elaine opened the other palm. "How about these, Henry?" She looked up at him, noticing that the distance between their two bodies had grown shorter.

"Dark red," he insisted, crossing his arms over his chest. He looked from one handful of berries to the next. "They are the same," he muttered, shaking his head in ignorance.

Elaine closed her eyes, inhaling a deep breath of tropical air, before reopening them. "No, they are not the same." She held the second palm of berries out before him. "Yes, they are both dark red, but these..." She motioned her head down to the red fruits in her right hand. "...mimic the color of an apple." Henry scoffed at that remark, turning his head away in frustration. "Now, which do you think are the poison, Henry?" Elaine held two open palms before him, set equidistantly apart. "The blood or the apple?"

Henry looked from one option to the next, left to right, then back again. Placing his palm against his chin, Henry touched the rough stubble of his new beard that had been growing in, now that he was no longer aided by the modern technologies of city life. He chose a hand, then carefully studied Elaine before revealing it to her.

"The blood," he uttered, convinced that Elaine would not have referred to these different berries as such unless blood signified the poisonous ones.

Without bearing any teeth, Elaine turned her lips upward, until they formed the half-moon shape of a smile. Then, while her eyes remained on Henry, she placed two of the blood red berries in her mouth and swallowed.

Henry panicked, his eyes widening in terror, as he grabbed Elaine by her shoulders, shaking her whole body. "What is the matter with you?"

Elaine quickly moved away from Henry, withdrawing from his grasp. She threw the berries in her left palm to the side, then tossed the other berries down at his feet. "It was the apple," she admitted, offering a treacherous, yet melancholy glare before turning away.

## Chapter 6

That evening, the moon appeared to rise much faster than any one before it. Henry had spent the rest of the day following Elaine around as she taught him how to collect coconuts from the island trees and spear fish in the sea. She was kind and calm in her teaching methods, and had not denied Henry the pleasure of receiving answers. But no matter how she carried herself later that day, Henry could not forget what had happened in the jungle.

Weeks passed and soon Henry had become another piece in the monotonous routine of a day spent on the island. He woke at sunset, though Elaine's cot was always empty when he did, and bathed in the ocean while she most likely did the same at the waterfall. Then, Henry collected stones, propelling them into the air as each coconut came toppling down, hitting the sandy ground by his feet. Afterwards, he searched the jungle for other fruits and nuts, making a morning meal out of all that he could find. He cut the coconuts in half and drank the milk of their fruity flesh to stifle the dullness of plain water.

By mid-morning, Henry ran the length of the beach twice, and then went swimming in the ocean, cooling his body down after so much physical exertion. At the end of his swim, just before reaching the shoreline, Henry caught two fish and collected seaweed from the ocean floor. The fish cooked well over the steamy fire that either he or Elaine tended to, and that, along with the seaweed, served as his second meal of the day.

Henry often rested after lunch, sleeping on the cot nearest the doorway. Before drifting off, he would gaze ahead at the vacant room and the empty cot against the far wall. Since their heated argument in the jungle, Elaine had kept her distance from Henry. He rarely saw her anymore, and was beginning to wonder if she had ever existed at all. Perhaps she was a ghost that his troubled mind had concocted after the traumatic shipwreck, to ease the pain of losing Charlie and nearly dying himself. And yet, just when he began entertaining thoughts of her ghostly existence, he would notice a garment of clothing strewn across the table or crumpled on her cot that had not been there the day before.

Elaine was real, and the truth of it was often more painful than if it had been a lie. Henry was stranded in paradise with a beautiful woman, but as the days wore on, he began to feel more alone than he ever had in his entire life in the city.

\* \* \*

Just past the third week of silence, Henry lay down on his cot, closing his eyes to partake of the regularly scheduled afternoon nap. Before drifting into a light slumber, Henry sat up on the bed, delighted by what he had heard – the sound of another's voice.

Henry slept with no shirt, and a pair of black trousers that fell against the ankles, so that is what he appeared in when he walked across the beach. Elaine ran along the shore with Jade, sloshing water with her frolicking, playful hands and feet. She wore a short light dress, similar to the others he had seen her in before, but this one was blue, more closely resembling the color of sky than of ocean.

"Elaine!" he called after her, walking across the sand, until their paths crossed.

Elaine turned around at the sound of her name, freezing in her tracks once Henry stopped before her. Jade sunk down into the sand, lying beneath the shade of a palm tree, as she rested her head against her paws, quickly succumbing to a catnap. Elaine gazed out at the ocean waves and accepted the fact that Henry had her cornered.

"Where have you been?" he demanded, scolding her as if she were his youngest daughter, who had left the house without saying a word.

"Here." She took her time with the word,

causing Henry's thinning patience to become more so. "The island," she explained, failing to turn her face and look him in the eye.

"I haven't seen you." He shook his head, resting his palms along either side of his waist. He could not finish the sentence, because that would involve telling her how much he had worried about her and searched for her and missed her.

"Yes." She looked down at the salty green sea foam, as the tide came in, splashing water against their feet.

At first, Henry felt relieved, but the emotion quickly returned to anger. After all this time, all these hours and days and weeks, just waiting to see her face, hear her voice, and this was all she had to say to him?

"It's been three weeks!" Henry yelled, trying desperately to pull her eyes closer to his, so that she would at least look at his face.

"What does it matter?" Elaine screamed back at him, turning her face to his, her eyes finally meeting his own.

In that moment, Henry noticed the faint outline of two scratches along the edge of her left cheek. He placed his palm against her jaw, running his thumb over the scratches. "What happened to your face?" Henry's tone drastically altered from outrage to concern.

"Nothing." She took his hand in hers and pushed it away from her face. "It's nothing," she insisted, turning her back on Henry.

"Did that creature do this to you?" Henry grabbed her elbow, turning her around to look at him. "Well did it?" He jerked her body in the process, upset by the prospect of any living person, creature, or thing laying a hand on her.

"No!" Elaine growled, violently pressing her hands into his chest to shove him backwards. She turned on her heel, walking towards Jade until Henry grabbed her by the arm again.

"Well then what did?" he demanded, looking down on her with a pair of stern, unrelenting eyes.

Rather than moving his hand away from her, Elaine placed her own along the top of Henry's arm. She held her lips together, only to keep them from quivering, as the faintest trace of a teardrop began to form along the edge of her right eye.

"There are creatures in that jungle that you cannot even begin to imagine." She placed her palm on the top of his shoulder before turning away.

"Elaine," he called after her, though did not move from where he was standing. "Elaine, what does that mean?" He watched her enter the shack, her slender, agile body moving through the white billowy curtain of fabric that hung over the doorway. Henry approached the entrance, but when he looked inside, discovered that Elaine had lain down on her cot, so he left her to sleep in peace.

* * *

Since it was no later than mid-afternoon, Henry entered the jungle alone, following the same path he had taken with Elaine on the day she had shown him how to hunt birds. He soon found himself standing by the waterfall and knew that the berries were not far away. When he came upon the first row of vines that ran along the ground, he picked a handful, placing them in the bowl he had brought from the shack. He knelt down, inspecting a single berry as he held the red fruit up to the light. "Blood red." He smiled.

Henry rose and continued along the path, noticing another section of red berries that looked extremely similar to the ones he now held in the bowl. He knelt down, studying a cluster of the tiny fruits, until he realized that each one had a small, minuscule line jaggedly etched across it. The lines resembled a network of veins, the way they break off and later connect again. Henry looked around the jungle in confusion. Why had he never noticed this before?

Pleased to discover something new, Henry tossed the berries in his bowl aside and collected the ones he had just happened upon. Since these berries had veins, he assumed that they were blood red. Therefore, the other berries he had just tossed from the bowl had been apple red, and, without a doubt, poison. Henry exhaled in relief, filling the entire bowl with the non-poisonous berries before returning to shore.

With his feet in the sand, Henry longed to swim in the water again before the day was through. The sun would not set for at least another hour, and Henry wanted to partake of as much sunlight as possible. So, he set the bowl of berries down beneath a shade tree, intending to wash and eat them later.

In the water, Henry felt renewed again, even as he first immersed himself among the rippling waves. He was tired from running and swimming and arguing with Elaine, so he floated on the surface, lying on his back atop the clear liquid. The sun shone down on his face, and Henry began to accept the fact that he would live and die on this island, for there was no way of getting home. Although, Henry no longer ached for the city the way he had before. He could not imagine himself in a happier environment, than the one he was already in.

"JADE!"

At the sound of Elaine's voice, Henry stood up in the chest-deep water, holding a hand over his forehead to block out the sunlight and see what had happened. After staring at Elaine and the panther for a moment, Henry swam to shore and made his way towards them.

"You," Elaine accused once she saw him surface the water. She marched towards him, shoving him to the ground as she screamed obscenities at him.

It was all one big blur to Henry, who lay in the

sand, staring up at Elaine and then looking to Jade, who also sat in the sand, catnapping as she had been earlier that day. "What is the matter with you?" Henry asked, still unsure why Elaine was acting so strangely.

"You tried to kill her!" Elaine shouted, slapping her hand against his bare chest when he rose from the ground.

"Kill who?" Henry brushed the sand off his back, looking around the deserted island for another female face.

"JADE!" Elaine gritted her teeth, nearly pulling her hair out as she stepped away from him to keep herself from truly attacking Henry.

"Nonsense," he declared, "I've been in the water this whole time." Henry pointed towards the sea, then motioned over himself to indicate the damp, dripping state of his body and clothing.

"Then what is this?" Elaine walked under one of the palm trees and knelt down to retrieve the bowl of red berries that Henry had placed there earlier.

"I picked them today. I was planning on eating them tonight." Henry slumped his shoulders forward, indicating that she was crazy for scoffing at such an innocent matter. When Elaine failed to move and only glared at him instead, he felt the need to say more. "Blood red right? You said I could eat these. They're not the poisonous ones, remember?"

"Ugh!" Elaine screamed out in frustration,

throwing the berries at him and then tossing the empty bowl to the ground. "I never showed you these berries." Elaine knelt down beside Jade, petting her back as the large cat began to purr.

Henry froze, suddenly realizing why the veins in those berries looked so unfamiliar. It was because he had never seen them before. They were a completely different type of berry.

"Are they poisonous?" he asked, growing less confused and more concerned with every passing minute. Elaine looked up at him, her eyes glazed over with tears, and offered a slight, yet definite nod. "How many did she eat?"

"I'm not sure." She gazed down at the panther and stroked her shiny black fur.

"Elaine, I'm so sorry." Henry knelt down, touching her hair. "I didn't know."

"Just leave us alone." Elaine stared into his eyes, not giving herself an opportunity to blink. When Henry had taken several steps back, she returned her attention to Jade. Elaine gripped the cat by the jaw and opened her mouth, though Jade began to struggle with her. "Jade, please," she begged, placing her thumbs between the incisors.

Elaine knew that Jade must have eaten at least a handful, so she had to remove whatever she could from the panther's mouth, and then nearly gag her, to make Jade vomit, and rid the poison from her body. Unfortunately, Jade was not interested in Elaine's intentions, though they may save her life. In order to show her defiance, the cat clawed at Elaine's face, so she ducked her head back before the cat's paw could touch her. But the powerful claws came down with brute force anyway, ripping into the flesh of her forearm.

Elaine fell back into the sand, shaking in terror as Jade opened her mouth wide, bearing her slimy fangs, as if she were ready to attack. Then, Jade closed her mouth and turned away, scampering off until she had disappeared into the jungle. Elaine felt frightened, for Jade had never shown any intentions of attacking her before. She looked down at her arm, drawing in quick, shallow breaths, as she noticed the bloody, gory mess of her skin. Red liquid began to drip against the sand.

Henry was at her side in an instant, but the image of him grew blurry very quickly. As she continued losing blood, a sense of unawareness came over her, until she slowly lost all consciousness. Henry acted in a hasty manner, cleaning out the wounds, and then ripping pieces of fabric from his own clothing to use as bandages for her arm. He carried her into the shack and laid her out on the cot, pulling a chair up to sit in front of her. He changed the bandages often, and began to worry that she was losing too much blood. But eventually the bleeding stopped, and Henry let out a sigh of relief in the darkness of the night.

He stayed awake as Elaine slept, brushing the pieces of dark hair from her face and wiping the sweat that accumulated on her forehead. She kept her brow furrowed, squirming every so often.

Henry wondered what she was dreaming about.

When she woke the next morning, Henry was by her side, offering her food and water as she asked for it, though she hardly knew what she was saying. The entire situation drained both of them, and Henry began to understand how Elaine must have felt when it had been him bleeding and unconscious in the bed. That night, Henry managed to climb into his own cot, nearest the doorway, but he did not stay there long. Elaine began to moan and whimper, and when Henry realized how much pain she was in, he rushed to her side and sat down in the chair.

"She's never done that before." Elaine barely opened her mouth to form the words, opening her fierce green eyes towards Henry. "She's never hurt me before." She rested her arm on the cot beneath her, slowly repeating the two sentences over and over again, like a mantra.

Henry leaned his face over her, pressing the back of his hand against her forehead. She was warm and clammy, still under a fever. "Elaine." Henry's voice silenced her, and she positioned her face to look up at his, though she had very little strength left. "We aren't meant to be friends with animals. It's not natural. Jade is wild." He brushed his fingertips against her cheek. "A predator. And it is not in her nature to like you."

Elaine looked confused, like she wanted to argue with him, but didn't have the strength to. So she gave into the weakness, letting her eyes close as she fell into a calm, yet restless sleep. With Henry's hand against the mattress, he leaned forward, placing a kiss on Elaine's forehead. He knew that she would neither feel nor remember it, but he did it anyway, knowing that it may be the only kiss he would ever get.

# Chapter 7

When Henry woke the next day, a splitting headache caused him to close his eyes, as the morning sunlight only made the pain worse. He looked over at the cot opposite his own, where Elaine should have been sleeping, but she was nowhere to be found. Then, as if reading his mind, she stepped through the doorway, with a box in her hands. The bandages over her forearm were damp with fluid, though she carried the heavy box to the table, as if it were no matter.

"How are you feeling today?" Henry sat up in the bed, the white sheet crumpled across his lap and over his legs.

"Wise," she spoke with her back to him. Elaine collected metal tools from the table - tools that Henry had never even seen before. She dropped each one into the box in a rhythmic pattern, paying no attention to the fact that each tool came crashing down with a loud thud.

Henry rose from the bed and walked over to

where she stood by the table. Looking over her shoulder, he noticed that she was placing building materials in the box. Elaine could feel Henry's body hovering around her, causing her to feel all the more infuriated. So, instead of delaying the news any longer, she told him what was about to happen.

"I want you off my island." Elaine turned around, only glancing in his direction for an instant, before passing through the filmy white sheet of fabric that hung over the doorway, and walked onto the beach.

"What?" Henry remained in the shack, too stunned to move. But then he grew angry, and followed her onto the shore. "*Your* island?" he questioned her, watching her every move as she set the box down beneath the shade of a palm tree.

"Yes, my island. I was here first." She stared into his eyes with a grim look in her own.

"Then what have I been this whole time?" Henry threw his arms into the air, frustrated that no matter what he did, Elaine could never be pleased with him.

"My guest." Elaine looked him up and down, studying the young man in his shirtless state.

"Well, where am I supposed to go, Elaine? This place doesn't have an entry and exit!" Henry rubbed his palm against the beard of his jawline, searching for her eyes when she began to ignore his.

Elaine slowly lifted her eyes up, gazing towards the ocean, and then offered a small nod in that direction. She left Henry standing alone, gaping at the crushing waves before him. He stood with his hands on his hips, trying to make sense of it all. Elaine returned to him, waiting by his side with something in her hand, though he was afraid to look at it.

"You can build a boat," she said, handing him an axe. "You have seven days." With a small, chiseled piece of rock in her left hand, she walked over to a slab of stone by the shack. Elaine held the piece against the slab and winced in pain, as she brought the writing utensil down with a thin tally mark, indicating that today would be his first.

When he saw her start to walk away, Henry went after her, grabbing her right arm, since he knew the left one was still tender. "What's the matter with you? You know it's nearly impossible to get off this island alive. Why, I nearly died getting here." Henry watched her fading expression as she looked down, refusing to meet his eyes. He placed his palm against her face and pulled her chin upright, compelling her to look at him. "What did I do? Whatever I did to upset you, I'll make it right, I promise." He wanted her to know that he was sincere, and that his intentions towards her had always been honorable. After all, she was the one who had been acting so severely towards him.

"I know you meant to hurt Jade, and I know

why." She placed her palm over his, as he rubbed his thumb across the small scrapes on her cheek. "But I can't have you here anymore. I'm sorry." She let go of his hand, and walked away until she had disappeared into the jungle.

Henry's eyes widened in alarm. He understood it now.

Elaine thought that Henry had set the berries beneath the tree on purpose, so that Jade would find them, eat them, and die. Elaine thought that Henry had seen the scratches on her cheek, attributed them to Jade, and then sought out a plan to eliminate her. Elaine thought and thought, but did she know?

Henry hadn't known that those berries were poisonous, but Elaine must have easily assumed that he had. Everything had happened in such an order that Henry could not explain himself away, or even lean on the truth, because Elaine would have every right to discredit it. In these circumstances, the truth was simply too unlikely to believe. So, accepting his fate, Henry slung the axe over his bare shoulder and entered the jungle to begin cutting wood.

\* \* \*

At the beginning of the allotted seven days of time, Henry and Elaine became strangers again. She rose before dawn, and by the time Henry woke, Elaine had been in the jungle for an hour. He chopped down a few trees, which provided him with enough wood to construct a small raft.

Henry knew a boat would be safer, but also more time-consuming, and now that he knew Elaine wanted him gone, he no longer wanted to stay on the island.

By the third day, Henry had lined eight posts of wood beside one another, and all that was left for him to do was tie them together. He searched in the jungle, looking for materials that he could use as rope to keep the posts side-by-side. At the same time, Henry was also in the process of constructing a small boat. He worried that the raft may fail in the water, especially since he would be traveling for such a long distance. So, he began building the base of the boat, and planned to have the raft finished by day four and the boat by day seven.

The sun beat down upon his back as Henry moved into the shade, wrapping the rope that he had fashioned from jungle vines around the raft. Out of the corner of his eye, he saw Elaine creep towards the stone slab, placing another tally mark beside the first two. Henry was surprised when she walked towards him and looked down at the raft in the sand.

"What is this?" Elaine wondered, kneeling down before him. Her long black hair hung down in loose waves, not far from her waist. She smelled of sweet flowers and passion fruit, compelling Henry to look up at her and inhale.

"I'm-" Henry stopped himself before he could form a complete thought. "What do you want

Elaine? I'm doing what you asked me to." He stripped a piece of shredding bark away from one of the logs. "Am I not doing it fast enough for you?" He had formed a sticky substance from coconut oil and an adhesive material he had retrieved from an insect's nest in the woods. Elaine studied him carefully as Henry began to coat each wooden piece with the substance, in the exact area where it would touch the log next to it.

"You only have a few days left." Elaine looked over her shoulder at the stone slab and its three tally marks. "I thought we could talk, since you'll be gone soon." She looked down at the sand, drawing pictures with her fingers, similar to the way a small child would. Henry noticed the sadness in her eyes, but was tired of her confusing emotions and nonsensical ways.

"I do *not* wish to speak to you." Henry stared into her dangerously beautiful green eyes, making a point to prove to her that whatever alliance they had shared, no matter how subtle it had been, was over. "Please leave," he exhaled, returning to his work as he finished gluing the last piece of wood to the raft.

"Jade is alive." Elaine placed her hand over the bandages. Henry noticed that fluid had finally stopped draining from the wounds on her arm. "I found her by the waterfall." Elaine looked over her shoulder, gazing into the jungle. "She must have not eaten as many as I thought, or..." she drifted off, pressing her fingers in the sand again.

Her brow furrowed as she tried to discern the picture she had made. "Well, she survived." Elaine gazed up at Henry, her lips held pouty and plump. Henry had mistaken her age for sixteen before, and she certainly looked it now.

"Elaine, what are you saying?" Henry brushed traces of sand away from the raft, then began to wrap the rope around the first two logs, squeezing them tightly together. "What? Now that I didn't kill your cat, you want me to stay?" He scoffed at his own question, turning the raft over to tie the rope into a knot at the back.

"I never said-" Elaine began, but then Henry interrupted her, his eyes still on the rope in his hands.

"No, you never said it. But you think I intended to kill her." Henry continued to tie the rope, twisting pieces of it into knots on the other end of the raft. "And I didn't." Henry brushed the sand off his hands, setting his finished product down, now that the raft was complete. But looking into Elaine's eyes offered a lesser sense of pride. "You still don't believe me, do you?" Henry watched her gleaming gaze falter, as her eyes slowly shifted, turning away. Not surprised, Henry rose from the sandy ground and carried the raft in his arms until he reached the water.

"Are you leaving?" Elaine rushed over to the edge of the ocean, letting the rough waves drown her feet in salt water.

Henry stood in waist-deep water, letting the raft

skim the surface beside him. "What does it matter, Elaine?" he shouted back at her, preparing to climb onto the raft. "When I want to leave, you want me to stay. When I want to stay, you want me to leave." Henry pulled himself onto the raft, sitting in the center to balance himself. But when the first wave that held any force came his way, water came rushing through the middle of the raft and split the wooden sections apart. Although Henry could not see it, Elaine firmly held her hands together on the shore and breathed in a sigh of relief.

## Chapter 8

That night, Henry woke to the sound of Elaine whimpering as she lay in her cot on the other side of the room. He pulled the white sheet back from his body and climbed down from his own cot, trudging over to her bedside. The day had exhausted Henry, and the large muscles in his arms were sore from chopping and carving wood. He was tired from head to toe, and the screaming tension in his back, chest, and abdomen, indicated that he was in need of a good night's sleep. And yet, Henry tossed his own needs to the wayside, for Elaine.

"Elaine." Henry shook her awake as she tossed and turned in the cot, her face twisting into a painful grimace. Her eyes opened in a panic as she clung to Henry, grabbing his arms to keep herself stable, as if all she had been searching for was something to hold on to. When she looked around and realized where she was, Elaine let go of him, embarrassed that she had behaved so strangely after waking up from a nightmare.

She quickly turned away and lay back down, her face looking towards the wall. Henry glanced at her back, noticing how it moved in time with the rise and fall of her chest. Elaine's eyes began filling with tears as she pulled the sheet up to her collarbone. Henry opened his hand to touch her arm, but thought twice about it and pulled back, sitting silently on the edge of her cot.

"Do you ever wonder why we ended up here?" Elaine spoke to the blank wall beside her, though the question was directed at Henry.

"No," he silently spoke, gazing down at her resting body. "Do you?"

"Yes." She pressed her little finger against the wall, drawing invisible images in the dark.

Henry exhaled, placing his hands on his knees. He looked through the small window by her bed and studied the full moon that sat peacefully in the night sky. "Does it matter?" Henry looked back at her, finding the point of discussion to be nothing more than meaningless.

"Yes." She sat up, prepared to look him squarely in the eye. "It does matter."

"Why?" Henry stood up, moving the chair that he had placed there last week, in order to give himself more space. "You can't do anything to change it." Henry paced the floor and crossed his hands over his arms as the night breeze drifted in through the thin tapestry over the doorway.

"Go lie back down, Henry." Elaine used her

thumb to sweep away tears as they collected beneath her eyes. "There's no use in talking to me." She pressed her cheek into her pillow, pulling the cover over her neck. Henry moaned in frustration, but was so overcome with exhaustion that he could not stand to be awake any longer.

To his surprise, Elaine was still sleeping when Henry woke the next morning. He dressed in the same pair of black trousers he had been wearing, though he had recently shortened them so that they fell just below the knee now. As he had been doing most every day, Henry left his shirt and shoes in the shack. But today, he entered the jungle, seeking out the waterfall where he had seen Elaine and fled like a frightened boy only a few weeks ago.

Once he arrived at the clear water, Henry knelt down, cupping the liquid in his hands and splashing it across his face. When the water calmed, smoothing into a clear pane, Henry was surprised by how quickly he startled himself. The image in the water could not have been his own.

His dark brunette locks had grown past the length of his shoulders, somewhat shaggy, though still relatively straight-looking. The smooth, delicate face that he once wore was now gone, and a rough, chiseled one, partially covered with thick beard, had replaced it. The pallor of his skin had never been terribly white, but now bore the resemblance to mud, the sun having browned every inch of skin Henry left exposed.

Nevertheless, his eyes were clear, and looked much the same, with the faintest bit of gold remaining along the edge of his irises.

Henry had not seen his reflection while on the island until now. As he gazed down at the water, Henry was surprised to admit that what appeared most unfamiliar to him were the physical changes in his body. He had always been tall, though lean, with a thin frame that retained less muscle than fat. But upon looking in the water, Henry saw a body that he did not recognize. A strong, muscular chest, with bulging biceps, and an abdomen containing deep, etched grooves that he had never seen on his body before. He looked like a gladiator in a Roman coliseum, or a Trojan warrior, intent on preparing for battle.

Not wanting to look at himself any longer, Henry slapped his hand across the water, causing rippling patterns to distort the image until it disappeared. Rising from the ground, Henry looked at the waterfall, lifting his head to take in the height of the natural wonder. He thought about scaling the rock that led to the top, just so he could jump once, and feel what it was like to fall. But that seemed like something a person would do when they had accepted the fact that their life was nearing its end, and Henry had yet to fall that deep into a vat of hopelessness.

When he returned to the beach, Henry retrieved the two pieces of his raft that had broken in half. He had placed them in the sun to dry yesterday and then pasted them back together with the sticky substance he had been using for glue. Since he would have to use the boat now, it occurred to Henry that he should make some use out of the raft, so he chiseled away the edges until it fit inside the doorway to the shack. By the time he began to attach the door to the small building, Elaine had already disappeared for the day.

He had always wondered what she was doing in the jungle or where it was exactly that she went every day. Just as he was finishing the process of attaching the makeshift door, Henry looked out across the beach, at a section of sand between the edge of the jungle and the palm trees. Henry placed his tools in the box Elaine had given him, and then ducked beneath the shelter of the shack, hiding just inside the doorway to keep himself from being seen.

The speck of darkness he saw that didn't quite match the light tone of the sand was a small wooden door. As it flung into the air, opening up a hole, Henry understood that it was a hatch, intended to keep others out. An arm opened the hatch, and as Henry looked closer, he saw long black tresses, and knew that it was Elaine climbing out of it.

When her feet reached the sand, Elaine looked over either shoulder and scanned the beach. Henry retreated farther into the shack, leaning against the nearby wall. He breathed a sigh of relief when Elaine closed the hatch, and then began to scoop piles of sand over it to cover the secret passage. Elaine rose, brushing the sand from her fingertips as she walked towards the water. Henry took the opportunity to sneak out of the shack and scamper into the jungle while Elaine's back was turned. She hadn't seen him.

\* \* \*

Henry began making his own tally marks in the stone, when the action no longer interested Elaine. She thanked him for the door that he had attached to the shack, saying that it would be useful during the rainy days to come. The weather was shifting, yet Henry could not let the black clouds or thundering booms in the night keep him from achieving the week's task at hand.

When Henry drew the sixth tally mark on the stone slab, it was to commemorate the completion of his boat. He had pushed himself beyond human limits every day, and even had time to fashion a paddle out of the remaining wood he had cut from the forest. But on that sixth day, just as Henry was preparing to leave the island, a raging storm washed ashore with the tide.

Elaine sought shelter in the tiny shack, shutting the door Henry had made for her, so she could secretly observe him through the window beside her bed. They had not spoken in days, and when she saw him push the boat into the raging tide, a silent tear slid down her cheek, caressing the space where he had touched her. Elaine looked on in fear as Henry sailed across the rushing waters, dipping the paddle on either side of the boat to keep from moving sideways.

Henry felt his body shudder as thunder continued to roll, turning the afternoon light into a black day. A bolt of lightning struck across the sky and sent chills down his spine. Henry gripped the paddle, pushing through the water, until a tremendous wave rose up before him, terrifying Henry until he had sailed over the incline, advancing into deeper ocean. Similar waves caused Henry's body to take on a normal amount of stress, until a powerful, rushing monster of a wave came flooding in Henry's direction.

With paddle in hand, Henry braced himself for the oncoming wave, paddling on either side of the boat to help him move past it. To his anguish, the wave was unstoppable in its unrelenting and gigantic glory, and so, Henry toppled out of the boat, as the violent water came crashing down, shattering the small boat to pieces.

Elaine ran onto the shore, despite the life-threatening weather, and clasped her palm over her mouth in mourning as she looked out at the horizon. She sank down onto the ground, letting the tide come in and soak her dry clothes. With her head in her hands, Elaine wept for him, reminiscing over the few smiles they had shared, and regretting the cold, silent days she had put him through. She buried her toes in the sand, as her face fell into her lap, grieving over the godsend that she had both mistreated and wasted.

After what seemed to be an hour of lifeless tears, Elaine felt a hard object press against her foot. Lifting her head from her lap, Elaine looked down, realizing that the tide was coming in, and bringing the pieces of Henry's tattered boat along with it. She collected each piece of broken wood as it arrived at the shoreline, making a stack in the fire pit. The stone slab caught the corner of her eye, bearing six tally marks on it. Hating herself, Elaine grabbed a chunk of wood from the pile and threw it at the slab, resenting every unreasonable demand she had ever sent Henry's way.

## Chapter 9

Farther down the shoreline, Henry felt the weight of nearly drowning wash over him as the powerful waves tossed him ashore. With his face in the wet sand, Henry lay flat on his stomach, digging his fingertips into the ground to pull himself upright. He was able to move his upper body forward, and pull his legs from underneath him, so that he could sit up. But as the tide came in, knocking against his back, Henry crawled towards the nearest tree, until he had placed enough distance between him and the raging ocean storm.

Henry lay in peace for only a moment, knowing that he must seek shelter soon. Turning his head to the right, he saw streams of smoke billowing into the air, though they were much farther down the shoreline than where he sat. A trickle of blood caught the corner of his eye as he discovered a large gash in his hand, assuming that when the boat smashed into pieces, one of the boards must have sliced his skin open.

Groaning in frustration, Henry rose to his feet, walking to the water as he dipped his injured hand into the burning salt liquid. The stinging pain in his hand was frustrating, but after all that Henry had been through, he did not care to recognize the discomfort. So, he turned, placing one foot in front of the other as he made his way towards the firelight in the distance.

Meanwhile, Elaine knelt down before the fire she had made, carefully placing each piece of Henry's broken boat into the flames. Since his body had yet to wash ashore, Elaine accepted the likelihood that he had probably been eaten by an underwater creature, and these pieces of the wreckage were all she would have to remember him by. As she placed her hand over the last shattered board, lifting it towards the fire, she paused, thinking that she should keep at least one piece of material evidence to prove that he had existed, long after she had lost her mind.

While Elaine remained frozen in motion, the last piece of the boat flew out of her hand, as if someone had batted it away. She looked over her shoulder, quickly rising to find Henry, alive and panting before her very eyes.

"What are you doing?" he shouted at her, despite the heavy rain that had begun to pour on them, soon silencing the flames by Elaine's side. "I need these to build another boat!" Henry gazed down at the fire pit, realizing that Elaine had turned all of the other wooden pieces to ash.

"I was using them for firewood," Elaine answered, too startled and frightened by his behavior towards her to admit the truth.

Henry glared at her, shoving his shoulder against hers as he walked towards the shack. Elaine followed him, unable to form words when she saw the glimmering axe in his hand. He trudged towards the nearest tree, the muscles in his arms and back screaming in pain when he lifted the axe over his shoulder, prepared to cut into the trunk of a palm tree.

"Stop!" Elaine stood near him, her scream interrupting the forward motion of his body. "Have you lost your mind?" Elaine moved closer, wrapping her hands around the handle of the axe to take the weapon away from him.

"I have to build another boat!" Henry complained, though the act of speaking distracted him from grasping the axe handle, and so it slipped out of his hands and into Elaine's. She trudged towards the shack with the object in hand, her black hair dripping, as the rest of her body became soaking wet from the rain. "Give me that!" Henry went after her, twisting her elbow at the entrance to the shack. She yelped in pain, though Henry ignored her. "I have to build another boat!" he repeated, grabbing her by the shoulders to make her understand.

"No, you don't!" Elaine brought her face close to Henry's, their eyes locking in one electric moment as a bolt of lightning struck the waves near the horizon in the distance.

"Listen to me." Henry leaned his face down before hers, so that it would be easier to hear each other over the thunderous weather. "I know you want me dead, and for some strange reason the storm didn't do its work. So give me that axe, Elaine." Henry stared into her eyes, already knowing that she would be nothing more than defiant towards him.

"No." She shook her head, turning on her heel as she entered the shack and attempted to shut the door behind her. But Henry caught the edge of the door with his heel and forced his way through, slamming the wooden makeshift door against its frame, as it locked the two of them inside.

"I see." Henry stepped towards her. "You want to finish me off yourself." Henry placed his hands on her shoulders and pulled her in front of him, despite Elaine's countless denials and protests. "So just do it," he said, repositioning the axe handle in her hand. Henry straightened the axe, wrapping Elaine's palms around the base and then stood still before her as he pressed the silver blade against his chest. Releasing his hands, Henry gazed straight ahead, puffing his chest out to make it easier for Elaine to sink the blade into his flesh. After a few silent moments, Henry looked down at Elaine, whose terrified eyes made her look all the more childlike. "No?"

Elaine released the axe, letting Henry take it

from her grasp as he walked towards the door.

"Then I'll return to the tree." He pressed his hand against the entryway, intending to chop enough wood to make another boat, regardless of the weather.

"You'll be struck by lightning," Elaine protested, moving a step forward as she crossed her arms over her shivering body.

"Precisely," Henry paused, looking over his shoulder at her. He pulled his lips together into a fine line, embellishing the nature of his high cheekbones.

"I don't want you to die," Elaine admitted, gazing at the back of his head as he stood before an unopened door.

Henry stepped back, turning to face her, overcome by astonishment and confusion. He let the axe handle dangle over his shoulder, before gravity pulled his arm down, forcing the blade to skim the surface of the floor. "Then why did you burn my boat?" Henry jabbed a thumb over his shoulder, motioning towards the window at the ash and smoke that remained from the fire. Walking closer to Elaine, Henry watched her eyes, as she struggled with herself, pressing her palms into her elbows.

"Because I don't want you to go." Tears brimmed along the edge of Elaine's eyelids, and as she gazed up at Henry, the first liquid drop descended, sliding down her soft golden skin.

Henry placed his thumb against her face,

brushing the teardrop away as he let his palm relax along the skin of her neck. As a brilliant flash of lightning struck against the shore, Henry bent his face towards hers and pressed his lips against her mouth. After that first kiss, Elaine exhaled, hesitating as she looked into his eyes. They were full of fear and wonder and light.

Elaine wrapped her hands around the back of Henry's neck, drawing closer to him as their lips met again. Henry placed his hands around her waist, slowly pressing her back into the wall. His lips traveled along her neck and jawline, as he picked her up in his arms and laid her down on the cot where she slept.

Henry lay down beside her, pausing for a moment to feel her heartbeat. He took a strand of her long, glossy black hair in his hand, and then pushed it above her brow, as it framed her face. Her vibrant green eyes looked resilient, beaming, and full of desire. He noticed that her hands were trembling, but when Elaine saw where his eyes were, she took one of her hands and placed it against his face, running her finger along his jawline. Henry wrapped his hand around her wrist and then moved close enough until the space between their bodies had vanished. With a gentle touch, he brushed his lips against her soft, supple skin, and in time, the couple had done what nature had always intended for them to do.

* * *

The storm had calmed when Henry woke in the middle of the night, looking down at the warm, empty space beside him. Rising from the cot, he gazed out the window pane, dressing in black trousers, as he studied Elaine's figure by the shore. Henry pulled his arms through a long-sleeved button-down shirt, whose white fabric glowed against his brown skin in the moonlight.

Walking across the sand, Henry felt each sinking step trying to pull him downward, like quicksand. He left the shirt unbuttoned, stopping just behind the patch of sand where Elaine sat, with her knees bent forward and the heel of each foot pressed into the sand. She held her arms around her stomach, not minding the outline of ocean water that crept towards her feet, traveling close enough to dampen her white dress every so often. The moonlight shone down on her honey golden skin, contrasting with the light-colored dress, in the same way Henry's skin had with his shirt.

Henry sat down beside her, pushing a mess of fallen hair over her shoulder. Elaine gazed out towards the ocean, though Henry's eyes remained steady on her face. She blinked for a moment, then studied the sand beneath her feet, the way the current came forward, and then rushed back out to join the vast, forceful ocean again. Henry shifted his gaze towards the sea, only turning back to Elaine once he noticed the faint glimmer of a teardrop streaming down her face.

"What's wrong?" Henry placed his hand against the back of her neck, feeling the warmth of her skin.

"We shouldn't have done that." She smudged the tear away in a forceful manner, as if she were ashamed that he had seen her cry.

Henry was speechless, and withdrew his hand from her body once he realized how indifferent she was to him. He studied the shadow of moonlight as it played against the moving waters. Rubbing his hands together, Henry let his elbows fall against his knees, before turning his gaze on Elaine again.

"Elaine, if I hurt you," Henry began, though Elaine shook her head, drying more tears. "I'm sorry, I wouldn't know..." Henry dug his heel into the wet sand. "I've never..." Henry bit into his lower lip, unable to look anywhere but down.

"You didn't." Elaine placed her hand against his arm, lightening Henry's spirits.

Henry turned his face towards hers, noticing the collection of more tears as their eyes met for the first time, beneath the moonlight. "Then why are you crying?" He placed his hand on her face, wiping the falling drops away, but she soon pulled his hand away with her own.

"Because we shouldn't have done it." She pulled her knees into her chest, resting her chin as she looked straight ahead.

"Why?" Henry searched her eyes, wondering

where the brave, dangerous, haunting young woman who had bludgeoned him with a stone had gone, and who this terrified, melancholy girl was that had replaced her.

"You wouldn't understand." She moved to stand up, but Henry grabbed her by the arm, pulling her back to the ground.

"Tell me." Henry stared into her eyes without blinking. "I want to know."

Elaine dug her fingers into the sand, drawing childlike images again, of the sun and moon and stars. "I'm not one of those girls," she crooned. "My parents were good people, and what we shared..." Elaine paused, having a difficult time trying to find the right words. "That was never meant for anyone but my husband." Tears brimmed along the edge of her lower eyelids. "What would Mother and Father think of me now? I'm the only one left." Elaine felt the need to hide, so she succumbed to her emotions and buried her face in her hands.

"Elaine." Henry combed his fingers through her hair, gently tucking a strand behind her ear. "Those things aren't important now. None of that matters." He wanted to lean down, and press his forehead against her own, but thought twice of it once she glared in his direction.

"How can you say that?" She pushed her hand into his chest, increasingly growing more defensive. "What I believe... what my parents taught me to believe, doesn't matter?"

Henry knew that he shouldn't have said it, because she would not understand. But there was no other way of explaining it to her, except by laying out the cold, hard truth. He could have been nicer, and told her these things in a more appealing way. But Henry didn't care how his words came across, not anymore, as long as they were the truth.

"No, not anymore," Henry breathed, searching for hope in her eyes, though he knew she wouldn't be able to see it. "Your parents taught you to believe in the right things, Elaine. They loved you." Henry took her face in his hands, thinking that if he pulled her closer, she would understand, she would see. "But marriage is based in society." He brushed a thumb against her cheek. "And we don't live in society anymore."

"What are you saying?" Elaine could not decide if she admired the way he spoke to her or resented him for it.

"I'm saying that what we did." Henry smiled, the light coming back in his eyes. "It wasn't wrong, unless you felt-"

"No," Elaine interrupted, "it was wonderful." She pressed her lips together, slightly biting the edge of her tongue in anguish.

"Then why are you torturing yourself?"

"Because it's not the way God wanted it!" Elaine screamed in Henry's face, her true anger leaking through. She looked away from him, not wanting her emotions to coerce her into acts of violence.

"How do you know what God wants?" Henry looked up at the stars, studying the way each glimmering spot contrasted with the black pane of darkness beneath it. "Maybe he's not even real," Henry mused. "After all we've been through." Henry's eyes danced across the island, thinking of the death, loss, and anguish in his life, and hers, since they both found themselves trapped on the island. "How can you be so sure he exists?"

A slight smile began to form at the corner of Elaine's mouth. Before rising to leave Henry alone on the beach, she placed her palm against his face, and said, "After the way you touched me tonight, how can you be so sure he doesn't?"

# Chapter 10

Two days had passed before Henry saw Elaine again. That night on the beach, she simply walked away from him, and Henry no longer had the strength to stop her. Elaine held her own independent thoughts deep within her, and trying to change those was like replacing the moon with the sun. It wasn't natural.

Henry stood over a pile of wood that he had chopped down in the jungle. He was cutting each piece into smaller sections that he could use to build a new boat. While chiseling away at the next wooden board, Elaine casually walked up to him, the nonchalance like a veil over her body. She was wearing the same soft white dress as two nights ago, and as she moved towards him with her hands over her arms, Henry could do nothing but stare.

"Henry." Elaine let her hands fall behind her back, twisting her palms at the wrist in hesitation. "I have something to tell you." She lifted her chin up, allowing herself to gaze into his eyes. Henry let his tools fall to the ground, and then brushed away the sand from his fingertips, motioning for her to continue. "I understand now." She looked fearful, intimidated even, by the way Henry crossed his arms over his bare chest, revealing the cuts of muscle along the side of each forearm.

"What do you understand?" Henry forced the question out, not wanting to dance around the subject matter with Elaine anymore.

"God." Elaine stared into the sand, before returning her eyes to Henry's, crossing her arms to mimic his posture. "He sent you here to be with me." The beginning of a smile formed at the edge of her lips. "So I want to."

"You want to what?" Henry had grown tired of her childish games in the days since she had abandoned him. He had slept alone, in Elaine's cot, the cot they had shared, too altered to return to his cot that lay on the other side of the room.

"To be with you." Her bottom lip trembled as she moved towards him, placing her palms against his chest. Elaine braided her hands together at the back of Henry's neck, and their eyes formed one unbreakable gaze.

"If things were different..." Henry let his hands lock around her waist. "If we were in New York, I would marry you-"

Elaine held a finger to his lips before he could finish his sentence. "You don't have to say it." Elaine wrapped her arms around Henry, hugging him closely to her body.

"I want you to know the truth." Henry rubbed his palms over her shoulders, lingering over the skin of her arms. With his chin against her back, he breathed her in, the scent a tropical, fruity breeze.

"I already do." Elaine pulled back, holding his face in her hands. She smiled before pressing her lips to his own, reassuring Henry that she was done running away from him.

\* \* \*

Later that night, Elaine lay beside Henry, pulling the white sheet over his bare stomach. Henry's arm lay draped over her shoulder as they talked beneath the moonlight, finally content in their honesty with one another. Elaine ran her fingers over Henry's jawline, stroking his scratchy beard.

"You remind me of my father sometimes." Elaine noticed the similarity, since she had seen no other man with such a thick amount of facial hair, with the exception of her father, during her time on the island.

"How?" Henry pulled his mouth into a grimace, staring at the ceiling until Elaine replied.

"You are wise, strong, brave." Elaine spoke in a serious manner, pausing between each word that she offered as a characteristic. "And so was he."

After a brief silence, Henry nodded to himself, then grew curious. "What happened to him?"

"My father?" Elaine only asked the question to

stall the inevitable. She knew what Henry had implied.

"Yes."

"He died." Elaine rested her head against Henry's shoulder. He could feel her breath against his neck.

"Yes, I know. But how?" Henry looked down at her, sitting up in the bed as he leaned on his elbow for support. Staring into her eyes, Henry tried to tease the truth out of her, but she quickly turned on her side, facing the wall, leaving Henry to gaze at her bare back. "Why won't you tell me?"

Elaine exhaled, feeling Henry's hand at her back. After a great deal of internal struggle, she finally relented, though kept her eyes on the wall. "He was murdered."

Henry pushed the fallen pieces of Elaine's hair over her shoulder, brushing his palm along her shoulder blade. "I'm sorry." He kissed her neck, placing an arm above her chest as he hugged her body close to him. "How did it happen?"

Elaine closed her eyes, not wanting to relive the painful memories, or see the gruesome look on her father's face again. But it was important that Henry know the truth, especially since he was living on the island. She could think of no better way to explain it to him, rather than to just begin, so she did.

"One night, I was chasing Jade in the jungle. She was only a cub then, and loved to run every place she could. When we reached the edge, where the sand begins, Jade stopped in her tracks. She was looking at something, so I knelt down beside her, and saw my father by the fire. But in the distance, there was a large ship with red sails, and it sat on the shoreline." Elaine placed her hand on the arm Henry had wrapped around her. "Three men left the ship, and walked towards the shack, where they saw my father by the fire. Two of them looked alike, dark hair, tan skin, perhaps they were brothers. But the third man, the blonde one, he was the tallest of them all. He was also the one whom I was most afraid of. At first, they seemed pleasant, and my father offered them food, but then the blonde one started shouting, saying that this place had been his island first, and that my father should leave."

Henry felt Elaine's pulse quicken beneath him, as he began to understand why she felt the way she did about the island. Brushing stray hairs away to expose the back of her neck, Henry wrapped his other arm around the front of her body, locking her in his grasp. Henry could sense what was coming and knew that she had lived in fear of it returning every day as the tide drew near.

"He stabbed my father, and I watched him die. I had to hold Jade back, because she was trying to run towards them, but we stayed hidden in the trees. They stayed on the island for three days, and then boarded the ship and left. I buried my father's body in the sand, on the north side of the island, and Jade was all I had left." Elaine rolled onto her other side to face Henry.

"And you were sixteen," Henry recalled, feeling her nod into his chest. "Have they returned since then?" He brushed his fingers through her hair, realizing, for the first time, why Jade attacked him when he appeared on the island.

"No," Elaine inhaled, closing her eyes with a yawn. "It's been five years and I haven't seen anyone but you." She soon fell asleep in his arms, but Henry had never felt more awake.

# Chapter 11

**H**enry rose at dawn, careful not to wake Elaine as he slowly slid out from under the white sheet. He watched her shift to her side, her hand tucked beneath the pillow. Dressing in the same white button-down shirt and black trousers, Henry left the shack, pulling the door closed behind him. While he walked beneath the rays of daybreak, Henry held a hand up to shield his eyes from the sun and looked along the shoreline to estimate the length of the beach.

Jade appeared from the bordering jungle, lithely stepping towards Henry as he held his hands out in a defensive manner. The cat stopped before reaching his feet, holding her mouth closed and jaw taut, staring at Henry with those beautiful, yet terrifying eyes.

"What do you want?" Henry boldly inquired, placing his hand over the knife in his pocket. He had found it among the building tools Elaine had given him, and been holding onto it for protection ever since.

Jade bent her head forward in a way that Henry could have sworn was a nod, and then knelt down in the sand, letting her long legs run parallel with the shore. Her sleek black tail stood up, slowly twitching back and forth, though only momentarily. Jade yawned, revealing a set of sharp, deadly fangs, before resting her head on her front paws and closing her eyes.

Henry stood in silence for a moment, still startled by her presence. He removed his hand from the knife in his pocket, and then moved backwards a step, to see if Jade would keep the posture. When she did, Henry walked sideways along the shore, not turning his back to her until he had moved well out of sight. Henry continued to trudge down the island, and at length, finally reached the edge, where land was no more.

Beneath one of the surrounding palm trees, Henry knelt down and studied a stone slab, similar to the one that Elaine had drawn tally marks on, resting over a section of sand. Henry brushed his hand over the stone, clearing away the bits of dirt that had collected over time. There was no name or date, but a small, yet recognizable cross had been etched into the center of the stone, denoting that the life beneath had been one of a believer. Henry looked back down along the shoreline, barely able to distinguish the small speck of black that must have been Jade.

When he returned, Elaine was playing in the

sand with Jade. A small bowl of nuts and berries sat on the wooden table by the shack, looking as though Elaine had nibbled her way through breakfast. Once she saw Henry approach, Elaine rinsed her hands off in the salt water, then dried them on the back of her dress. "Are you hungry?" She approached Henry, pulling at the collar of his shirt as she planted a kiss on his lips.

"Yes." Henry accepted the bowl of fruit and nuts in her outstretched hand, ravenously shoving handfuls into his mouth. Elaine handed him the pitcher of water, which he gladly took, draining it dry in the time it took Jade to enter the jungle.

"Where did you go?" Elaine rubbed her hand over his shoulder, looking deep into his eyes. Henry placed the empty bowl and pitcher on the table, running a hand through her hair.

"I saw your father's grave at the end of the island." Henry looked over his shoulder, pointing along the shoreline, into the distance.

"Yes." Elaine held a hand up to shield her eyes from the sun, acknowledging the place where she had buried her father.

"I'm so sorry, Elaine." Henry grabbed her by the waist and pulled her body close to his. Elaine rested her chin on Henry's shoulder, not feeling the desire to say anything more about her father's death. "I think it would be best if I build another boat." Henry leaned out of the embrace to look her squarely in the eye.

"Why?" Elaine's brow furrowed. She could

not bear the thought of him sailing into the ocean again, after what had happened on the night of the storm.

"Well, those pirates could come back at any time. And if they do, we need to be ready." Henry left her side, and then returned with the box of building materials, sharpening the blade of his axe.

"Ready for what?" Elaine placed her hands along her hips, feeling the bitter taste of an argument brewing between them.

"Ready to escape." Henry knelt down in the sand and began unloading the tools from the box. "To leave the island if we have to."

"The sea would kill us." Elaine stared down at Henry, sure that there was no other way of understanding the matter.

"And the pirates wouldn't?" Henry smirked, removing a knife made for chiseling from the box.

"Why do you keep calling them pirates? I never said they were pirates." Elaine crossed her arms over her chest, holding her jaw together in a taut, unwavering position.

"Well." Henry haphazardly slung a tool he didn't need into the box. "My darling, pirates are what they very well may be, from the way you've described them to me."

Elaine felt soft on the inside at the sound of Henry calling her his "darling." She thought the matter over again and realized that Henry was only being cautious, in case the men did return.

"I'm sure they see this island as their own,

Elaine, no matter how much you may believe it is yours." Henry rested the axe against his shoulder, turning to look at her with a calm, but serious nod, before heading into the forest to cut more wood.

Elaine stood with her arms crossed over her chest, gazing out at the crisp blue waters. She jerked her chin upright in a defiant, unyielding manner, studying the horizon as the salty breeze tossed and twirled her raven black hair in the wind. Digging her toes into the wet sand, Elaine relaxed her arms so that her hands clasped tightly around her elbows. She looked over her shoulder to find Jade approaching from the jungle. The cat lay down on the ground beside her, looking up at the hidden, terrifying blackness in Elaine's eyes. The tide was turning, and the dark sea was drawing closer.

\* \* \*

Henry cooked his fish over the flames, watching the moon make its slow ascent towards the center of darkness. He tore the meaty flesh of the sea creature apart with his fingers, offering pieces to Elaine as each became roasted enough to make the fish palatable. Despite the night sky, Henry kept a careful eye on the hatch in the sand, not a quarter of a mile from where he was sitting with Elaine, in front of the fire. It was not difficult to sneak glances towards the secret passage that Elaine had yet to share with him, since she could not stop staring at the red-orange flames at their feet.

Later that night, Henry lay sleepless on the cot, unable to ignore the sound of crushing waves that grew restless against the shoreline, matching the thuds of tree branches that battered against the window. Elaine rested on her side, moving a strand of black hair away from her face, her back to Henry. She could feel his breath on her neck as he leaned down over her, placing his hand against her arm to see if she were awake. Elaine closed her eyes, embellishing every exhale to offer the illusion that she was asleep.

Henry slowly slid out from underneath the covers, careful not to wake her as he stepped into a pair of boots. Buttoning a cool white shirt over his chest, Henry set out into the night, gently closing the door behind him. Elaine lay still for several minutes, until she had silently finished counting to a hundred, and then pulled the covers back.

She crept towards a wooden cabinet against the far wall and opened a secret drawer that appeared to be nothing more than a decorative panel. Reaching her hand into the drawer, Elaine felt in the dark for a medium-sized dagger that her father had always kept there for protection. As her fingers traced over the open space, Elaine grew frantic, realizing that the dagger was gone.

Elaine rose from her crouched position on the floor and shut the drawer with a quick movement. Turning around, Elaine slammed into the cabinet once she noticed a dark figure in the doorway that had begun creeping towards her. The man was tall, with long, shaggy blonde hair that fell to his shoulders. He was holding the dagger in his hand, moving closer to her as the blade collected flecks of moonlight, the shimmer betraying its place in the darkness. She collided with the wooden table and pushed it towards the man to protect herself from his violent intentions. But he shoved the table aside, grabbing her body with one hand. As he threw her in the air, her body crashed down on the wooden table, and she woke up.

Henry's hands were on her shoulders as she sat up in the cot, catching her breath. Elaine looked around the room, discovering a wooden table that had not toppled over, and began to wonder if the dagger was in the cabinet. Henry placed his palm against her cheek and felt how warm she was, hoping that she had not developed a fever. Elaine sank into his embrace, rested her chin on his bare shoulder, and folded her arms around his back.

"Are you all right?" Henry pulled out of the embrace, so that he could look her squarely in the eye.

"Yes." She nodded, shifting her eyes towards the cabinet. Henry traced his thumb over her lower lip, leaning in to kiss her. "Henry." She stopped him, placing a palm against his chest. "I must show you something." She moved around him, leaping down from the bed, then opened the secret cabinet drawer, where the silver dagger lay glimmering in the moonlight. Elaine grabbed the weapon, clutching it at the center of her palm, until her wrist felt flexed and tight.

Henry pushed his arms through the sleeves of his white button-down shirt and ran a hand through his unkempt locks, as he followed Elaine through the doorway. Elaine held a firm grip around the handle of the dagger, slowly treading through sand before she reached the border of the jungle. Henry kept close behind, noticing the way the moonlight illuminated Elaine's white dress, causing the fabric to glow against her skin. Her black hair hung down past the middle of her back, its glistening sheen akin to the panther's fur coat.

Henry followed Elaine into the forest, constantly twisting his head from side to side to beware of the wild creatures Elaine had spoken of. He walked beside her, moving branches and other greenery out of their path with his hand. As he pushed a worrisome tree limb away from Elaine, Henry was startled by the sight of a green snake that had coiled itself around the branch. With its slithering tongue and beady black eyes, the snake twisted in a circular nature, descending the length of the tree limb. Henry grabbed Elaine in his frightened state and ran into the night, pushing the couple deeper into the jungle.

Elaine burst out in laughter once they had reached the waterfall, clutching her stomach at the tolerable pain caused by her incessant giggling. She pointed at Henry, whose chest rose and fell, while he attempted to retrieve what breath he had left. "You've been in the city too long," she declared, giggling as he playfully nudged her shoulder, demanding that she stop.

A deep, cat-like prowl emerged from the woods, quickly growing closer, as Jade moved through the trees, pouncing from branch to branch. Threatening sounds rose up from her throat, worrying Elaine, who looked back at the sight of the big, black jungle cat, walking overhead along a stout tree limb. The cat stuck its claws into the side of the wood, dangling over the branch to hiss and growl at them, bearing a thick, sharp set of white fangs.

Elaine studied the physical body of the creature, noting the long, muscular back, and stout, wide shoulders. There was a jagged edge to the end of its tail, as if another animal had bitten through the skin, pulling a piece of the panther away with it. Elaine's eyes raced back down the length of the creature's body, settling in on the large, obtuse shape of its head. A dull pair of silver eyes sat like diamonds in luster, roughly positioned between the panther's forehead and snout.

While her eyes remained on the wild creature, Elaine shifted, placing her free hand against Henry's arm. "Run," she softly commanded, tightly gripping the dagger in her hand.

Henry's eyes darted from the panther to Elaine, then back again. "Why?"

"That's not Jade."

Elaine took off running, soon passing the waterfall. Henry kept pace with her, looking over his shoulder at the black panther that remained at their heels. He leapt over rocks and tree roots, ducking to dodge the occasional branch that hung down too low. He felt Elaine running beside him, her hot breaths audible in the air. The big black cat remained on their heels, chasing them deep into the darkest parts of the jungle. Henry looked back, over his shoulder, terrified by the cold, violent gleam in the panther's eyes.

The predator's glare distracted Henry, causing him to trip over a bulging network of tree roots and fall to his feet. But even then, the panther kept on, chasing Elaine into the night. Henry quickly rose to his feet, despite the pain in his knees and hands. Rushing towards the nearest tree, Henry cut a low-hanging limb with the knife in his pocket and carried it with him as he chased after the panther that was still chasing Elaine.

When the panther's tracks ran out, Henry looked to the right, noticing that Elaine had climbed up a tree, and the panther was clawing his way up the bark, not far behind her. Henry wrapped both hands around the tree branch, whacking the animal across its hind legs, but that only made the panther scale the tree that much faster. Elaine crawled out onto an elongated branch, peering down at the ground below. A shudder crept over her body, forcing the hair to rise up on the back of her neck. If she were to fall at this height, it would surely kill her.

Elaine squatted down on the branch, bracing herself, as the panther came creeping towards her with slick, hot saliva dripping from his upper fangs. With each step the panther took, Elaine cried out in panic, for the bending limb could not support the weight of the male creature, and was about to snap. Realizing that the dagger was still in her hand, Elaine held the weapon out, ready to defend herself. When the panther moved closer, Elaine thrust the blade into the air, missing the animal with every attempt. The panther batted its large, sharp-edged paw in her direction, cutting into the skin of her arm. Elaine yelled out in protest, swatting the knife against the panther's face, though she skimmed no more than the outline of his thin, protruding whiskers.

The black panther placed a stout, bristly paw before Elaine's feet, forcing the branch to descend further. Elaine winced at the sound of snapping wood, because she could feel the tree limb beginning to detach from its trunk. Staring into the panther's glistening silver eyes, Elaine was no longer frightened by the way his large, wet tongue moved across his teeth. She held her arm in the air, just beneath eye level, bending it at the elbow, so she could protect her face. Then, with the dagger gripped firmly in her hand, she swiped the blade across the creature's snout, finally connecting with his body. The panther stepped back, bearing his fangs at Elaine, as she noticed blood oozing at the gash across his nostrils. From her crouched position, Elaine swatted at the panther's snout again and again, pushing him towards the tree trunk, until he was finally forced to retreat.

The panther scaled the length of the tree and landed on solid ground before fleeing into the night. Elaine kept her posture firm and still, as the branch jostled in reaction to the panther's departure. Slowly inching forward, Elaine steadied herself, gazing down at the vast, vertical stretch of space below. Elaine inhaled, taking another step before the branch snapped in half. Her feet fell out from under her, as she stretched her free hand out towards the remains of the branch. But there was not enough wood left to allow for an easy grip. So Elaine's hand slipped from the limb, and she descended into the humid night air.

# Chapter 12

**E**laine felt her body softly gliding through the air, slowing the landscape around her into one blurred motion. The light skirting around the bottom of her dress billowed outward, circling in the pattern of a carousel. A small breath escaped her parted lips, as she reached her hand out, catching the top of a tree limb. Elaine looked down in disbelief, panting at the sight of her dangling feet, that had become suspended in the air, while her left hand clung to the rough, scraping bark above her. She stabbed the dagger into the trunk of the tree with her right hand, positioning herself at an angle that made it easier for her feet to reach the nearest outer-hanging limbs.

Balancing herself, Elaine released her hand from the branch above her, gently easing her way around the base of the tree. She tugged at the handle of the dagger, struggling until she was able to remove the blade from the hole it had made in the wood. As she sat down on one of the lower-hanging limbs, Elaine placed the dagger in her mouth, biting her teeth down against the handle, in order to free both hands for climbing. Elaine could feel the pull of weight against her muscles as she swung her arms out and leapt towards the next set of tree limbs.

Every ounce of energy had been drained from Elaine's body, as the inner part of her limbs became fatigued. When she reached the lowest branch, Elaine closed her eyes and then took a long moment to exhale, removing the dagger from her mouth. She pounced onto the wet forest floor and let her arms dangle by her side. Searching the surrounding woods, Elaine felt her eyes falling downward, at the base of a tall, bulky tree, not far from the one she had just descended. Henry lay face down, with his limbs extended outward, and his head turned towards the side in a gruesome, unsightly manner.

"Henry." Elaine stumbled, barely able to find her feet on the way over to him. She collapsed at his side, overcome with terror at the sight of his lifeless body. Henry's mouth hung open, his frozen face embellished by the ghostly appearance of his glassy brown eyes that stared into the distance, as if they had been haunted by some frightening, otherworldly creature. "Henry, Henry, Henry..." She repeated his name like a mantra, lying down beside him, as she rubbed her hand against his shirt, his face, his hair.

As Henry lay in dead stillness beside her,

Elaine ran her fingers along his skin, tracing the outline of his jaw and cheekbones, then rested her palm at his chin, to feel of his beard. She moved her hand along his arm until she reached his hand, squeezing his rough, dirty fingers with her own. Elaine was disturbed by the manner in which his hand lay against the earth – solid, yet unable to be pressed completely flat. Tugging at his wrist, Elaine turned Henry's hand over, exposing a poisonous arrow head, whose point remained stuck at the center of his palm.

Elaine brushed a few pieces of brunette hair out of Henry's eyes, noticing how silent and immobile they remained. Kneeling down before Henry, Elaine pulled the skin around his palm taut and removed the piercing dart from his flesh. She placed the dart in a wide bowl-shaped leaf, setting it aside as she turned Henry over and laid him down by the flat of his back. Pressing her ear against his mouth, Elaine listened for slightly muted breathing, but heard nothing of the kind. She placed her lips against his, breathing into his mouth for several second intervals, trying to determine exactly when the paralysis had taken effect.

Elaine remained by his side throughout the night, breathing for him at such a continuous rate that her mouth and lungs had grown sore. She rested her head on his chest when he began breathing on his own again, remembering a similar encounter with her father as a child.

The first year on the island, Elaine had yet to grow accustomed to the wild, dangerous nature of the bordering jungle. Without her father's permission, she crossed the border where the jungle met the sand, and ran through the wilderness in exploration. It wasn't until her bare foot came down on something sharp, painful, and needle-like that Elaine truly feared the forest, beneath its majestic layer of exotic wonder.

After that day, Elaine was aware of the poisonous darts that were scattered in hidden places all throughout the island. At thirteen, she believed others inhabited the island, and had planted the poisonous darts as a means of trapping and killing intruders. She did not learn the true purpose of the darts, or the origin of their maker, until the night of her father's murder.

In the years leading up to his death, Elaine's father warned her of other dangers in the wild, placing emphasis on the fact that even the smallest creatures could prove deadly, such as the vibrantly-colored frogs, who were the actual producers of the poisonous venom that had entered Henry's system.

When his fingers began to move at sunrise, Henry blinked, slowly sitting up as his eyes scanned the jungle landscape around him. He opened his palm, rubbing a finger over the spot where the dart had pricked his skin. Ruffling a shaky hand through his hair, Henry began to remember what had happened the night before.

He saw the images, as they flickered through his mind, in sharp, biting flashes of light and dark, pulsating through him like an irregular heartbeat, starting and then stopping again.

The sight of Elaine's dangling body in the tree had made Henry feel more agony than the moment Charles's body had floated towards him in the ocean. That liquid force of nature had been an engulfing power that nearly drowned all of them, and Henry had already been plagued with guilt for not having the ability to save at least one. But Elaine was an entirely different scenario altogether. She was the only person on the island besides him. How could he fail at protecting her?

"Elaine," Henry called out, raising his voice, despite the dry, raspy discomfort at the base of his throat. "Elaine," he repeated. The action grew tiring very quickly, so Henry lay back down, shifting to his side as the crushing reality overcame him – he had lost her.

As the first tears began to form, Henry placed a hand over his eyes, furious with himself for not having the will to save her. He felt a cool palm against his forehead, coaxing him and calming him. Henry took the hand and jerked it away from his face to find Elaine seated before him with a pitcher of water in her hands. Elaine placed her hand at the back of Henry's neck, helping him lean his head forward, as she placed the brim of the pitcher to his lips.

Henry moved his lips, as if to form words

between each drink of water, but felt as though he didn't have any strength left. Elaine began to stand up, intent on retrieving more water after Henry had drained the pitcher, but he grabbed her by the wrist, begging her to stay with no more than his eyes. Succumbing to Henry's wishes, Elaine lay down beside him and rested her head against his chest. Henry touched her arm, careful not to hurt her as he examined the newly cut gashes from the night before. The five claw marks were long, thick, and equally spaced apart from each other.

Similar markings rested along Elaine's forearm, where Jade had scratched her only days before. Henry laid his head back, staring up at the soft patches of blue sky that formed among the tree branches. With a protective arm wrapped around Elaine, Henry hugged her body to his, gently caressing the skin of her arm. It had remained soft and smooth, despite the recent panther attacks.

Once Henry regained his strength and mobility, he began telling Elaine of what had happened the night before. When the panther climbed down the tree, it collided with Henry, knocking him to the ground. Henry moved his hands out to catch himself as he fell face forward and landed flat on his stomach. As he pressed his palms into the ground to help him rise to his feet, the dart pierced his flesh, sending poison through his veins.

Elaine listened to Henry's heartbeat as he

spoke, noting the way it developed an irregular pattern when he mentioned the poison. In time, Henry drifted off, falling into a deep, exhaustive sleep. Elaine sat up and placed her palm against his chest, as she moved her fingers down, outlining every cut along his abdomen. She spread her fingers over the claw marks on his stomach, matching her hand print to the size of the panther's paw. Then, she placed her hand along the claw marks covering her own body, paying special attention to the bloody paw print she had received last night.

Sighing to herself, Elaine gazed down at Henry's troubled state of sleep. She tucked her feet beneath her legs and brushed the hair back from Henry's face, in order to feel his forehead. Elaine eyed the jungle territory surrounding her, knowing that another predator could very likely approach them at any minute. But Henry barely had enough energy to move, and she could not bring herself to wake him, just to test his strength, when he was resting so peacefully.

Elaine clung to Henry, startled at the sound of screeching monkeys in the distance. A pair of the restless, manic creatures swung from branch to branch, passing through the trees, until one of them stopped, turning its rounded head to observe Elaine. She sat motionless, too terrified to move an inch, even preventing herself from breathing too deeply, so that it would not notice the dramatic rise and fall of her chest. The monkey kept still, staring at her, before turning its head away, and following the other monkey through the tree tops, each swinging a pair of long, hairy arms from limb to limb.

Catching her breath, Elaine watched Henry sleep, relieved that the screeching monkeys had not been loud enough to wake him. For the first time in years, Elaine was terrified at the thought of remaining on the island. It had been Elaine and her father for some time, then he was gone. Now Elaine had Henry, but how long could they both last on the island? She had cheated death so many times in recent months, and so had Henry. It was only a matter of time before one of them wouldn't make it out alive.

## Chapter 13

S even days passed before Elaine entered the jungle again. Henry had returned to his work, chopping and carving wood for a new boat, in case they should ever need to leave the island. Elaine was pleased that Henry had fully recovered from the effects of the dart poison. His rehabilitation was a blessing that she had not taken lightly.

In the late afternoon, Henry took a break from constructing the boat and searched for the water pitcher to quench his thirst. He stood over the table by the shack, surprised to find empty bowls with a few specks of mashed banana remaining, but no water pitcher. Henry peered into the doorway of the shack, but Elaine was not inside, as she had been only moments before. An uneasy feeling crept over Henry, as he stepped back in the sand, scanning the deserted beach before him. Trusting his instincts, Henry slung the axe over his shoulder and made his way towards the jungle.

Meanwhile, Elaine weaved her way through the

intricate trails of the wilderness, clutching the water pitcher with one hand. She kept her eyes forward, constantly searching for any sign of danger. A pair of long-beaked birds flew overhead, gently landing on a brittle tree branch covered in leaves. Their feathers were coated with vibrant blues, yellows, and greens, except for the black-and-white stripes that surrounded their coal black beaks.

Elaine paused to watch the birds, mesmerized by their exotic look and natural behavior. All was quiet and peaceful in the jungle, as she closed her eyes, listening to the rushing waterfall in the distance. The silence broke at the sound of a creature's piercing cry, and Elaine opened her eyes, fearfully searching the landscape before her. The birds flew away in a rush of blurred color, fleeing from the black panther that drew closer, pouncing from tree to tree, as it pursued one of the monkeys Elaine had seen the week before.

Turning on her heel, Elaine ran through the wilderness, dropping the pitcher from her hand as she escaped the predator and its prey. Seeking shelter beneath a gathering of palm fronds, Elaine watched the panther bat its paw against the back of the monkey's head, as the smaller creature fell to the ground, whimpering out in agony. Elaine turned her head away, cringing at the sight of the panther's jaw clamped around the monkey's neck. Thick droplets of blood dripped down to the monkey's stomach, sopping its brown, bristly fur with the dark, gruesome evidence of death.

With the monkey dangling from its mouth, the panther turned around, eyeing the palm fronds that kept Elaine hidden. As the panther stalked towards her, Elaine held her breath, feeling the ground around her for a weapon. Biting into her lip, Elaine remembered that she had left the dagger in the shack and thrown the pitcher on the ground. A rare breeze swept over the forest, jostling the palm fronds that covered Elaine. She ducked down farther, her thighs burning with pain, but the sudden motion pushed some strands of greenery away, exposing Elaine's long black hair.

The panther froze in place, terrifying Elaine as she shrieked out in horror. Surrendering, Elaine knelt down, tucking her head between her legs, until she heard the panther's subtle footsteps. With fallen pieces of hair in her face, Elaine watched in relief as the panther walked away. The panther looked back at Elaine, revealing a pair of glassy green eyes. In that moment, Elaine realized that the panther was Jade.

\* \* \*

Elaine collected the water pitcher from the stretch of grass where she had dropped it, and continued through the jungle until she reached the waterfall. Kneeling down before the pool of water, Elaine dipped the brim of the pitcher into the clear liquid, gazing up at the falling waters before her. Before she could fill the pitcher completely, the black panther emerged from the shadows of the forest and stalked towards Elaine.

"Jade." Elaine beamed, relaxing at the sight of her animal companion. Once the pitcher was full, Elaine placed it on the ground beside her and cupped her hands into the water, splashing the cool moisture over her face. Elaine placed her palms along the edge of her scalp, wetting her hair with the water that remained on her skin. Looking at her reflection, Elaine pulled her fingers through the ends of her hair, loosening the tangles that had formed while hiding beneath the fronds earlier. After she turned away from the glassy liquid pane, Elaine stumbled backward, startled by the defensive, masculine nature of Jade's slimy snarl. Upon closer observation, Elaine's heart began to pound, for above the sharp white fangs, Elaine noticed a pair of silver eyes, and the gashed nose that sagged beneath them.

Henry stepped out from the shadows, holding the axe handle loosely in his hand before slapping the sharp blade against the side of the panther's face. The animal staggered away from Elaine, keeping his head down. Elaine lay on the ground, with her legs sprawled out, and her hands firmly placed in soil. Gasping for air, she felt weak and lightheaded, as if her body might collapse at any moment. Henry swung the axe at the panther's back, striking the creature repeatedly, even when he heard the sound of crushing bone. The panther cried out, his black muzzle peeling back over his sharp fangs as he growled in agony.

Blood sprayed over Elaine's legs, sprinkling her white dress with droplets of crimson liquid. "Stop," Elaine protested, crawling towards the creature. "Henry! Stop!" She tugged at the hem of Henry's shirt, noticing that the panther's body had gone limp. But Henry continued to beat the creature, accidentally elbowing Elaine in the jaw, as she flew backwards, collapsing onto the ground.

Henry held the axe above the panther's body, bringing it down with one final blow, until he realized that the animal had not moved for several minutes. Tossing the weapon aside, Henry knelt down and opened the panther's jaw with his hands. Its tongue hung loosely to the side, as the panther made no effort to breathe. Instead, it lay there silent, motionless. Henry had killed the panther.

Rising to his feet, Henry turned to Elaine, finding her on the ground, with a shaky palm clutched to her chin. She was crying. Henry knelt down to console her, but quickly discovered that the closer he moved to Elaine, the more terrified she became. "Don't cry, Elaine," he pleaded with her, noting the splattered blood on her dress. "I killed it." He tucked a strand of jet-black hair behind one of her ears. "I killed the beast." He sat down beside her, wrapping a protective arm around her shoulder.

"Well if that's a beast, then you're a monster." Elaine removed her hand from her jaw to push Henry's arm away from her. When she exposed her jaw, Henry noticed a trail of blood running down her neck, and realized that her chin had been split open.

"Did that creature do this to you?" Henry titled her head up, wiping the blood with the tail of his shirt.

"No." Elaine stared directly into Henry's eyes, while heavy tears brimmed from her own. "You did."

Henry rocked back on his heels, looking over his shoulder to make sure that the panther was truly dead. Elaine held her head in her hands, sobbing at the sight of Henry. His hands were covered in blood, and splotches of the thick red liquid adorned his face as if he were a savage. There was even a trace of blood on his lips, and Elaine could not bear to look at them, remembering how soft and delicate they had felt the night before. How could they have been the same lips?

"Elaine," Henry beckoned, tugging at her wrist to pull her near the water, where they could cleanse the blood from their skin and clothing. "I protected you from that creature." He stood up, walking over to the panther's corpse. "I saved you." He looked back over his shoulder at Elaine, then knelt down at the pool of water to wash his hands.

Even though she normally would have, Elaine could not muster the desire to thank him. "What will you do with him?" Elaine remained seated on the dirty earth, not minding that her dress and face were muddy, or that her arm and chin were throbbing in pain.

"Perhaps it would be best if we wash our clothes afterwards." Henry pulled his hands from the water, wiping them on the back of his shirt – the only part that remained white. "Here." Henry grabbed the panther's two front paws, wrapping an arm around each of its wrists. "I need you to help me drag it." He jerked the panther back, with its belly facing up.

"Drag it?" Elaine rose, uncomfortably watching the panther's head bob against the ground between Henry's feet.

"Yes," Henry huffed, too exhausted from his work with the axe to continue stressing his muscles. "We won't have to hunt for weeks." He dropped the panther against the ground and turned back to Elaine with an impatient look in his eyes.

"You want to eat him?" Elaine pointed at the animal, disgusted at the sight of blood oozing over black fur.

"Why, of course, my darling." Henry used his shirt sleeve to wipe the sweat collecting at his brow. Elaine trudged over to the dead body, leaning forward to press her hand against his abdomen, legs, and arms. She knelt down by the creature's chest, placing her palms on either side of his face. Touching the soft ears, wiry whiskers, and furry face sent a chill along Elaine's spine. His coat felt just like Jade's.

Elaine opened the panther's mouth, pressing her finger against one of the sharp fangs. She had always wondered what those pointy teeth felt like, but Jade had never been comfortable with letting her touch them. Elaine rubbed her thumb over the gash in the panther's nose, thinking of the blade that had placed it there. Gazing into the panther's stone cold eyes tortured Elaine, so she placed her hand at the creature's forehead and shut them.

Henry touched Elaine's shoulder, startling her as she moved away from him. "I frighten you?" He assumed the words as if Elaine had never spoken them, as if she had never said anything at all.

"Yes." Elaine hardly kept her mouth open when she answered, for her throat had turned dry.

Henry shook his head, deeply offended by what she had said. Pacing the ground before the dead panther, Henry widened the distance between them to make Elaine feel more comfortable. "I would never hurt you." He gazed at Elaine from where he stood, placing his hands on his hips. The way she looked at him nearly pierced a whole in his heart. He thought about the dart poison, deciding that it had been less painful.

"You already have." Elaine pressed her palms together, braiding her fingers as if she were about to say a prayer. "I want you to bury him." She rose from the ground, marching over to Henry as the fear left her eyes.

"What? But we need the food-"

"I don't care!" Elaine interrupted, her face nearly touching Henry's. Her eyes fell as she stepped back, looking over at the panther one last time. "If you eat..." Elaine shut her eyes, not able to finish her thought. "...that kind of meat, you may wish to do it again. And what's to stop you from hunting Jade?"

"I wouldn't!" Henry placed his palms on her face, trying to make her see reason. But Elaine pulled away, repelled by the touch of his hands. Henry's face crumpled in anguish, as he began to realize that Elaine could not bear to be that close to him. He longed to touch her, hold her, protect her from any threat that may appear. But he could not protect her from himself.

# Chapter 14

S tars had begun to decorate the night sky with sharp, glimmering specks of light, by the time Henry finished digging a hole. The panther's body was thick with muscle, but Henry dragged the creature past the waterfall, deciding that it would be best if he buried it deep in the jungle, in a place that Elaine would not suspect. Henry struggled with digging the hole, since he had no shovel, and the only tools he could use were designed for building. Yet, somehow, Henry managed to dig a pit that was plenty deep for the creature's body to fit comfortably.

Lifting the panther over his shoulders, Henry tossed the limp body into the hole, unnerved by the sight of its paws sticking outward once it hit the earth. Including its tail, the panther spanned the length of eight feet, which became more visible once Henry looked down at the wide hole. Henry stared at the panther's face, determined that its eyes would open once more, even though they had not since the creature had stopped breathing. Tossing soil into the pit, Henry filled the hole until it became a mountain of dirt, eventually rising to ground level.

Henry brushed the dark soil from his hands, collecting his tools before heading off into the night. Longing for redemption, Henry desperately hoped that Elaine would realize that he had saved her from the beast, and that it had only been a predator of the wild, sooner to eat her than befriend her. But Jade shared the same breed with the beast, and that subtle truth caused Elaine to loath Henry for killing one of Jade's kind, even if it had been to protect her.

Though he had not yet reached the waterfall, Henry could already make out the faintest traces of smoke in the air, as it billowed atop the trees. A slight curve formed at the corner of his mouth, while Henry bit the edge of his tongue, relieved that Elaine had stayed near the shack, and not hidden in the depths of the jungle, as she had been known to do. Henry decided that he should clean the blood and dirt from his clothes once he reached the waterfall, so he would appear more presentable when he saw Elaine. Henry wanted nothing more than to please her, to show her how much he cared. But as their time spent together wore on, it was becoming a much more difficult task to implement.

Trudging through the jungle, Henry wondered why he had not come upon the waterfall yet.

Enough time had gone by for him to have reached the falls by now, yet they were nowhere in sight. In fact, he could not even hear the rushing waters from where he stood at present. Pausing, Henry looked from side to side, scanning the territory around him, though could not grasp a sense of direction. Shrugging his shoulders, Henry convinced himself that he was close enough to the beach. He would not have been able to see smoke rising from the fire otherwise.

Stepping forward, Henry looked down in frustration once his feet became stuck in a pile of mud. "Wonderful," Henry griped aloud, noting that he would have to clean his boots now as well. But as he lifted his leg, the viscous substance clung to his feet, causing Henry to sink still further into the ground. Henry stretched his arms out, reaching for the hard, reliable ground that surrounded the mud. But every effort to free himself only forced Henry deeper into the mud. It was not until the sticky slime reached his thighs, that Henry realized he was being swallowed whole by a bed of quicksand.

"Elaine!" Henry screamed for her in the night, praying that she would be able to hear his voice. "Elaine! Help me, please, Elaine!" Henry cried out, frightened as the suction around his legs grew increasingly painful. The quicksand coated the lower part of his body, hardening like cement. Henry could barely tolerate the constricting force, once his legs began to pulsate. "Elaine!" Henry sighed in relief when she appeared before him, gasping for air. Elaine was still wearing the white dress, even though it remained splattered with blood.

"Henry." Elaine ran to him, devastated to find that he was standing in quicksand that engulfed him from his hips down.

"No." Henry waved his hand in the air, not wanting her to fall in as well. "Stay as you are."

Defiant by nature, Elaine disobeyed, stepping towards the quicksand. "Take my hand." She lay down on her stomach, still safe on solid ground, while she reached her arm out towards him. Henry leaned his body forward, brushing his fingertips along her palm. Elaine wrapped both of her hands around his, pulling with all of her strength. As she did, Elaine's body began to slide towards the quicksand. She was losing at Mother Nature's game of tug-of-war.

"Stop." Henry pulled his hand from Elaine's grasp, begging her to step away before she came too close to the quicksand. "The axe!" Henry motioned towards the weapon on the ground beside him, watching Elaine hurry to grab the axe by its wooden handle.

Turning the object over in her hands, Elaine pointed the end of the handle towards Henry, as she held the space of wood just beneath the blade in her grasp. But with Elaine pulling the axe away from Henry to get him out, and Henry pulling the axe towards himself to do the same, he descended into the quicksand even more, as the muddy substance rose to his waist. Henry yelled out in anger, glancing at the gathering of blood stains along the axe's handle and blade.

"I never should have buried the beast." Henry turned on Elaine, unable to force the bouts of rage that had been building up inside of him to subside. If he had dragged the creature to shore, and cooked it over the fire, and eaten the meat, as he had originally intended to do, none of this would have ever happened.

"What?" Elaine pulled the axe away from Henry before he could drop it into the quicksand. She stood over his sinking body, wiping any traces of the muddy slime onto her dress.

"You were the one who demanded that I bury the filthy creature, after he nearly flayed you alive." Henry could feel the quicksand pulling his body down, using more force when he attempted to free himself. "Have you nothing to say?" Henry glared up at Elaine, unsure if he was holding his jaw taut for the purpose of arguing with her or defending his life. With the axe in her hand, Elaine turned on her heel, walking away from Henry. "Where are you going? Come back here!"

Elaine approached a nearby tree, holding the axe above her head, before she came down on the wood with a cutting blow. Though her arms were screaming in pain, Elaine brought the axe down several times at the crux of a thick, low-hanging tree limb, in the space where it met the trunk.

Once the branch was detached, Elaine walked over to the safe ground that bordered the quicksand.

"Hold on to this, until I come back." Elaine set the branch down, indicating for Henry to place his hands around it. Henry grabbed the branch with one hand, and then snatched Elaine's wrist with the other.

"Do *not* leave me here, Elaine." Henry gritted his teeth together, so overcome with anguish that he nearly pulled Elaine into the quicksand with him. But she jerked her hand out of his grasp, stepping backwards before she ran into the night, unable to escape the lingering sounds of Henry calling her name.

## Chapter 15

E laine raced across the sandy beach, collecting rope and pieces of broken board from the raft Henry had built some time ago. Throwing the rope over her shoulder, Elaine clutched the wood in her arms, quickly crossing the border that led into the jungle. Henry's wailing screams could be heard for miles. Elaine was sure of it. Though Elaine had noticed a glimmer of abandonment in his eyes, Henry would not drown in the quicksand, unless he let go of the branch. The only reason Elaine thought he might ever resolve to that, would be if he had given up completely. And Elaine knew that Henry was not one to surrender so easily.

When Elaine reached Henry, the quicksand had risen to the space just beneath his chest. Tossing the boards to the ground, Elaine knew that she had to act fast. So, she cut the rope in half, then tied a portion of it in a circle around Henry's chest. "You came back," he weakly murmured, surprised that she had not abandoned him.

"I told you I would." Elaine knotted the rope at his side, looking into his eyes. Henry was wearing that troubled expression – the one that always came over him when he wanted to kiss her.

Elaine grabbed two of the wooden boards from the ground, placing one behind Henry so that it pressed against his back, and the other in front of him, so that it pressed into the skin below his chest. Both boards lay horizontally flat, though were long enough to touch the border of solid ground at either edge of the quicksand. Elaine guided the line of rope towards a thick tree branch, where she tied the remainder of the rope into a resilient knot. Climbing over the tree branch, Elaine planted her feet into solid ground and began to pull.

Elaine tugged the rope towards her, though the task was not an easy one. As she pressed her body into the stout limb before her, Elaine gritted her teeth, relying on the only strength she had left to pull Henry from the quicksand. Henry placed his palms over the wooden board that pressed against his chest, utilizing the platform for leverage, as Elaine had intended.

"Don't fight against it," Elaine commanded, knowing that the more Henry struggled, the more powerful the suction would become. So, Henry relaxed his body, releasing the will to struggle with the murky, constricting substance.

With her arms burning, Elaine continued to

pull the rope, though it had begun to irritate the palms of her hands. Heat spread through her body, until drops of glistening sweat were running down her face. Despite every pain in her body, Elaine could not stop. She would rather die than relinquish Henry's body to the quicksand.

When Elaine feared that she could no longer hold on to the rope, Henry's feet finally emerged from the muddy pit, as she pulled his entire body out. Henry crawled on his hands and knees, collapsing to the ground, once he was free from the quicksand.

After cutting the rope from the tree limb, Elaine rushed to Henry's side, removing the rope that she had tightly wound beneath his chest. Henry could hardly breathe, holding his hand over his heart to feel its pounding rhythm. Elaine struggled with Henry's body weight as she tried to lift him to the ground. Placing her hands beneath his arms, Elaine pleaded with Henry, until he had risen to his feet. Elaine slung Henry's arm over her shoulder, steering him in the direction of the waterfall. But Henry resisted, unable to do anything more than keep his feet firmly planted on the ground.

"Elaine, I can't," Henry moaned, barely able to keep his eyes open. The throbbing pain in his legs and stomach weakened Henry's resilience. He simply did not have enough strength left.

"Stop that, Henry," Elaine muttered, struggling to support the bulk of his body. She was nearly out of breath herself. "Find your strength." She fought against the screaming pain in her back, dragging Henry along with her, though in weight, his body was twice the size of hers.

Once the pair reached the waterfall, Henry sank down at the edge of the pool, bringing Elaine to her knees. She bent her head down, peeling his arm from the back of her neck. Elaine knelt down before the water, splashing the cool liquid over her face. With Henry nearly unconscious at her side, Elaine began to remove his white button-down shirt. She was sure that the quicksand had formed a paste around his body, coating any exposed skin that had not been covered by clothing. If Elaine did not wash the constricting mud from Henry's skin, it was only a matter of time before the pulsating throb of the quicksand began to damage his flow of blood and oxygen.

"Come on, Henry." Elaine jerked at the buttons that formed a line down his shirt. Alarm jolted through her once she realized that quicksand had crept beneath the white cloth. Mud covered the majority of his upper body.

Elaine tossed the shirt on the ground beside them, not bothering to remove the rest of his clothing before submerging Henry into the water. He hardly had the strength to keep himself afloat, but the pool was relatively shallow, with water reaching no higher than the space just below his chest. Elaine swam out towards him, grateful that Henry could stand on his own two feet. With her hands at his back, Elaine positioned Henry's body beneath the falling water, steadying him as the rushing rapids beat the murky mud away.

Henry felt a sense of relaxation come over him, once the water had removed every trace of quicksand from his body. He blinked several times, only for the sake of flushing any bits of remaining grime out of his eyes. Cupping his palms together, Henry smoothed his damp hair back, in order to see what lay before him.

At the sight of Elaine, Henry stood still, letting his wet hands dangle at his sides, beneath the cool water.

Elaine stared into Henry's eyes, realizing that he had woken up from his weak, drowsy spell of lethargy. Moving closer, she placed her palm against his bare chest, content to see that his heart was still beating. Henry could not look away from Elaine, mesmerized by her appearance as she wrapped her arms around him, hugging his body close to hers.

Water sprayed onto the couple from above, though neither noticed. Henry rested his chin against Elaine's shoulder, sighing at the smell of her black lustrous hair. Squeezing her gently, Henry soon found his hands at the curve of her waist. He locked his hands together behind Elaine's back and held her in his arms.

Looking out into the night, Henry took several deep breaths, realizing the peril that lay waiting for them in the jungle. It would not disappear, and would not falter, yet there seemed to be little that could be done about it at present. Pulling back, Henry held Elaine's head in his hands, with his fingers gently wrapped around her neck. Elaine looked into his eyes expectantly, as if he were her elder, her protector, her lover. Henry leaned forward, pressing his lips to her forehead, before Elaine folded into him, resting her head in the space between his neck and shoulder. In the warmth of the night's embrace, Henry proudly accepted his fate. No matter what trials lie ahead of them in the jungle, Henry was never letting her go.

## Chapter 16

L ying beside Elaine that night, Henry wrapped a protective arm over her stomach. Henry's greatest desire was to shield her from harm, no matter what the cost. As she looked into his eyes, Elaine placed a hand against his bare chest, tracing her fingers over the scars along his stomach, which closely resembled the marks on her arm. Now, it was plain to see that Henry and Elaine had more in common than their place of origin.

"Tell me, Henry." Elaine laid her head back on the pillow, studying the line of his finely taut jaw. "How come you never found yourself a wife?" Elaine pulled her fingers through the ends of his dark, shaggy mane.

"I suppose I was never interested." Henry looked at Elaine's mouth, noticing the way her lips spread over two rows of straight white teeth.

"In ladies or marriage?" Elaine sat up in the cot, letting Henry's hand fall from her stomach so she could pull the cool white sheet up to her collarbone.

"Marriage." Henry's brow furrowed as he realized what he had said. Elaine would denote an entirely different meaning than the one he had intended, as had been known to happen between the two of them in the past. But the word had already come out, and there was no way of retrieving it now.

Elaine pulled her lips into a fine line, holding her jaw taut. Turning onto her side, Elaine faced the wall, with her back to Henry. She felt a hollow space in her chest, overcome with disappointment at the sound of that one word Henry had uttered. A tear glistened at the corner of her eye, before the drop descended, gliding against the smooth, golden texture of her skin.

"Elaine." Henry placed a hand on her shoulder, resenting himself for causing her to worry about foolish things. But Elaine remained stiff, unwavering, even as Henry begged her to listen. "You misunderstand me entirely." He pulled his hand away from her, understanding that she did not wish to be touched. "I meant what I said, that day on the shore." Henry was angry with himself, especially since Elaine had just pulled him from a pit of quicksand that could have very easily taken his life.

"No, Henry." Elaine turned towards him, only revealing the side of her face. Henry noticed the faintest trace of a teardrop on her cheek. "I understand. You are a man, and I cannot expect you to be any more than that." Elaine clasped her hands beneath the pillow, wanting nothing more than to rest. Silence filled the shack, as no other word was uttered for the remainder of the night. Henry lay awake, staring at the ceiling, though a careful eye remained on Elaine's sleeping body.

Of all the ways he could have explained his circumstances in New York to her, why had he chosen those words? Truthfully, he had never been interested in marriage, because he had yet to meet a girl who was worth marrying. Try as she might, Henry's mother had been unsuccessful at finding him a proper match, because she had always chosen girls like Emmaline Winters and Abigail Ellis.

To escape the everyday complaints of his mother, Henry had attended fishing and hunting trips with Charles as often as possible, avoiding the weekend dances and surprise house guests. Even then, when Charles had sought out nightly taverns to pay for his share of time with the ladies upstairs, Henry had always disappeared, slipping out through the back door. Charles had always been too intoxicated to notice, so Henry would walk home alone, sometimes distracted by the view of rustling curtains from the tavern's second story window. Yet, the diversion would not keep him long, no more than the amount of time it took for him to scuff his boot against the pavement. Then, Henry would stroll the streets of New York City, mindlessly wandering through Central Park when the thought of entering his family's home at such an early hour was dreadful enough, with his mother and her maddening disposition to periodically enslave him during a fit of marriage talk.

All of New York came rushing back to Henry in a faded blur, until he finally dozed off before the early morning light. When Henry woke in the late afternoon, he felt sluggish and stiff, as if he had been beaten with a wooden stick. The space beside Henry was cold and empty. As he placed his palm over the cot, Henry assumed that he had been lying there alone for most of the day.

Elaine had risen at daybreak, just after Henry finally fell into a deep, restless sleep. When Henry walked along the beach, calling out in search of her, Elaine kept quiet, for she was below ground, beneath the hatch in the sand.

The cellar boasted many secrets that Elaine had yet to share with Henry. Shelves lined the walls from floor to ceiling, storing countless bottles of wine and rum. It had all remained the same as the day Elaine had arrived on the island, except for the one bare wall that was covered with thousands of tally marks, denoting the amount of days she had survived on the island.

Once Elaine was done counting, she carved a star beside a cluster of five tally marks, then made the same mark by another. Stepping back, Elaine stared at the slashes along the wall, lifting her fingers to her face to wipe away the tears. Elaine heard Henry's voice again, calling her name, so she folded the small pocket knife in her hand and hid it behind a wine bottle on the seventh shelf from the top.

Elaine placed her foot on the bottom step of the ladder, looking back at the wall before she climbed to the top. Once she reached the hatch, Elaine flung the wooden panel open, revealing herself to Henry as she had never done before. Henry stood no more than ten feet away from Elaine, though he did not act surprised. Elaine stepped onto the sand, shutting the hatch behind her.

"Don't look so stunned," Elaine bitterly scoffed. "I know you've seen this before." Henry looked down, resting his hands on his hips. It was true, but had he told a lie? He had concealed his knowledge of the hatch from her, but so had she. "And I know you saw me bathing at the waterfall, some time ago." Elaine dropped piles of sand onto the hatch, patting and spreading the fine granules out, until the wooden panel was invisible.

"I'm sorry, Elaine." Henry searched for her eyes, longing to see the deep jungle green. He wanted to be assured that she was still the same woman. "I hadn't intended for that to happen," Henry hesitated, staring at the back of her head as she walked away, "either time."

Elaine turned back to him, realizing that it had come to this. "I need to show you something, before the sun sets." She had intended on revealing all of her secrets to him the night they had been chased by the panther, and since then, every attempt to do so had been met by another life-threatening catastrophe.

"Wait." Henry grabbed Elaine's arm, turning her body around so that she would have to face him. "I need to tell you something, about last night." Henry let go of her arm, swallowing before he went on. "You are lovelier than any woman I've ever known." Henry cupped her chin with his hand, stirring a delicate sensation within Elaine. "All my life, I never knew how it could be," Henry gasped, as if he had been searching for air. "All my life," he repeated, "and I never knew, Elaine." Her fierce green eyes met his, quickly calming before they grew somber and morose.

"Henry." Elaine studied his handsome, chiseled face, keen on resisting the distraction. "I *must* show you something," she stressed, as if it were a matter of urgency.

"Elaine," Henry complained, indicating that he was not yet finished explaining himself.

"I know." Elaine placed her palm over his. "I understand what you meant before," she sympathized, offering truth among her secrets, "and I believe you."

Henry exhaled in relief. He had not expected her to be either forgiving or understanding. But he was glad nonetheless, and took her in his arms before she could utter another word.

Elaine grabbed Henry by the hand, tugging at

his wrist in an impatient manner that he was not accustomed to. Leading Henry into the jungle, Elaine remained as silent as a stalking creature in the night, though golden sunlight filtered through the trees. When they reached the waterfall, Elaine jumped into the lagoon, confusing Henry as he waited before the border separating water from land.

"Come on," Elaine yelled over her shoulder, floating in the water just before the falls. Henry gazed across the pane of clear glassy liquid to find Elaine as beautiful as ever. Strands of glossy black hair fell against her back, while her skin glistened in golden hues, shimmering beneath the rays of sun that had dared to pass through the trees.

Henry removed his shirt, tossing the white clothing on the ground before plunging into the water. He swam towards Elaine, pulling her body close to him. Elaine's white dress was sopping wet, causing the material to cling to her skin. Henry picked her up in his arms, wrapping his hands around her back as if she were a small child

"Henry," Elaine scolded, freeing herself from his grasp. She swam beneath the falls, disappearing before Henry's eyes. He followed her, pushing his body through the rushing water. Behind the cascade, Henry discovered a flat gray surface made of slate, that protruded outward from a hidden cave. Elaine lifted herself onto the smooth slab, wringing water out of her hair and clothing while she waited for Henry.

"What is this place?" Henry pulled himself up, kneeling at the edge of the stone floor before standing beside Elaine. Searching the rock wall that stood before him, Henry noticed black markings etched into the surface. A dark passage lay to Henry's left and right, resembling a forked pathway, except for the wall of rock in between them.

Elaine disappeared down the first passage, with a wooden torch in hand, cheerfully smiling at the sight of Henry running after her. When she struck the wooden stick against the stone wall, her face lit up beneath the glowing flames.

"Where are we going?" Henry followed Elaine through the tunnel, growing leery as the path curved away from the sunlit entrance. "Are you going to answer any of my questions today?" Henry watched the outline of his shadow against the cave walls, wondering if he looked that tall in the daylight.

"Be patient, love." Elaine held the torch out with her left arm, exposing a sleeping bat that hung upside down from the ceiling of the cave, with wings enfolding its body like a vampire's cape. Henry wrapped his arms around Elaine's waist, stealthily sneaking behind her until they had passed the bloodsucking creature. Elaine giggled at the way Henry used her body as a shield to protect him from the small animal.

Elaine turned at the end of the tunnel, climbing a narrow case of stone steps. When she reached the top, Elaine led Henry through another passage and up additional steps, their bare feet scraping against the rigid surface. At the end of the tunnel, Henry saw a light that continued to lengthen and expand, until they walked into an open cavern. Elaine approached the edge of jagged rock that they were standing on and peered down at the water below.

"What is this place?" Henry shouted over the rushing cascade before them.

"It feeds the lagoon," Elaine yelled over her shoulder. She lunged forward and leapt over a wide stream of water, whose path descended over the edge of the rock, forming an indoor waterfall.

Henry crept near the edge and gazed down at the steep drop below. Even though the water would catch him, Henry had no intention of falling. So, he jumped over the rivulet, just as Elaine had done, and followed her down another set of stone steps. When he looked back at the rushing water, it no longer seemed deadly from a distance.

"Hold this." Elaine handed the glowing torch to Henry, as he clasped the base with one hand. She stopped in front of an old rusty door, and then looked over either of her shoulders.

"Where are you taking me?" Henry demanded to know, feeling uneasy in the cavernous enclosure. Despite the large ceilings and echoing chambers, Henry felt near-claustrophobic, since his feet were not firmly set on land.

"You are the most impatient man I have ever known." Elaine flitted her green eyes in Henry's direction, which only made him feel less aware of his surroundings.

Henry parted his mouth in surprise, when Elaine pulled a silver key from her breast and slipped it into the lock on the door. The key hung from a chain around her neck, which Henry had never noticed before. Elaine twisted the handle and pushed the door open, as they both stepped inside.

Elaine pulled the key chain from the door, then shut it behind them. Henry watched her slip the necklace over her head and tuck the key into her dress. When Elaine caught Henry gaping, she took the torch from him and began strolling through the room.

Following closely behind, Henry nearly staggered over at the sight of gold coins. Abundant gold coins that filled nearly the entire room. Among them were precious stones: rubies, emeralds, and diamonds alike. The glistening gems sparkled beneath the light of the torch, a rainbow of jewels in the dark.

"Good God, Elaine," Henry exhaled. "Where did such a lot come from?"

"I can never be certain," Elaine answered. "But I believe the whole lot came from those men." Her eyes turned downcast, staring at the treasure.

"The pirates?" Henry wondered.

"The men who killed my father," Elaine

clarified.

The sight of those beautiful, valuable, tainted jewels made Elaine's blood boil. She would love nothing more than to see it all burn, until nothing remained but ash.

Henry waltzed over to the treasure and skirted his hand across the top, causing a number of gold coins to slide down the mountain of wealth and spin atop the floor. Overjoyed, he tossed his hands in the air and soared into the pile, landing in the middle of the treasure. Elaine glowered at Henry, while he dug his fist into the jewel covered mound and scattered the stones and coins about. The way he played in the treasure made Elaine writhe with anger. But she managed to suppress her temper successfully, until he found a golden crown, a king's crown, and placed it on his head.

Boiling over with rage, Elaine snatched the crown off Henry's head and flung it across the room. Henry glanced up at her, recognized the fire in her eyes, and stood up. The couple held steady eye contact, as Henry shook the coins and jewels from his clothing and approached Elaine.

"Have I done something to upset you?" he asked, reaching for her hands.

Scowling, Elaine withdrew from him and fled the room, only allowing enough time for him to exit, before locking the door behind them.

"Elaine!" Henry yelled over the rushing water. But he hadn't spoken soon enough to stop her before she slipped the key chain around her neck and dove into the water.

Watching her swim away felt like a knife in his chest, so Henry jumped off the edge and went after her. His eyes burned, as he opened them beneath the water, chasing Elaine's escaping figure up ahead. Henry had never held his breath underwater for so long before, and when he finally surfaced in the lagoon, the familiar outdoor waterfall to his back, his lungs felt like they were on fire.

Elaine had already climbed out of the water and was ringing her long black locks out by the edge of the lagoon. Gasping for air, Henry stood up until the water came to his knees, then reached out and grabbed her arm.

"Ah!" Elaine cried out in surprise, as Henry jerked her back into the water with him.

"Speak to me," Henry growled. "What have I said? What have I done?"

Elaine turned her face away from his, not wanting to uncover his flaws. Quite frankly, Henry should have known precisely what it was that he had done wrong.

Henry planted his fingers around her jaw and pulled her chin back, until her face was mere inches from his. He gazed into her vibrant eyes, deep as the sea, steady as the night, green as the jungle. She was the only woman who had ever been suited to spar with him, to test him, to enrage him. Henry had traveled nearly half a world away, without which he might never have known her.

But Elaine had been well worth the trip.

"Tell me," Henry coaxed, holding her face in his hand.

Elaine clamped her teeth together and looked down. Then, when she knew that Henry wasn't going to surrender, Elaine glanced up. "I hate that treasure," she seethed. "And I hate those men!"

Elaine broke free from Henry's grasp and stepped out of the water, her dress dripping wet. Henry watched her walk away, studying the lines and curves of her figure through the garment, until she disappeared into the jungle.

# Chapter 17

Henry found Elaine in the ocean, bobbing chest-deep before the waves. Desperate, he treaded across the sand until he reached the shoreline, and then swam out to meet her.

As Henry approached Elaine, her eyes remained on the horizon. He had found her looking this way many times before, but had never asked the purpose of such a ritual. Even now, when Henry was floating beside her, within arm's reach, she would do no more than stare straight ahead, out at the horizon. Henry kept his eyes on Elaine, willing her to give him the slightest glimpse, but she would not.

"We have to leave," Elaine announced, her voice as serious as ever.

"Leave?" Henry blinked at the same time he furrowed his brow, sure that she must have been joking. "What on earth do you mean?"

"We have to leave the island," she declared, honest and forthright.

"Why would we do that, Elaine?" Henry kept his head above water, as distant waves sent a rippling current towards them.

"They return to the island every five years. I found an old calendar once, and a map, both of which belong to them. They come back every five years," she reiterated. "And they take more treasure with them when they go. That's why they killed my father. They thought he had found it, too."

"Had he?" Henry probed.

"No," Elaine gently lilted, the brief utterance hardly making a sound.

"Then how come you have that key?" Henry pointed to the silver chain around her neck, as his eyes drifted downward, to the place where she had hidden the key between her breasts.

"One of the men must have dropped it in the sand, because that's where I found it the day after they left."

Henry followed Elaine's blank stare and gazed out at the horizon. All he could do was imagine a young Elaine, secretly tucked behind the cover of the jungle, clutching a panther cub in her arms. She must have died a thousand deaths at the sight of her father being murdered. Henry had witnessed Charles and the captain and all of the crewmen drowned, but he could not fathom the degree of pain and anguish and suffering that Elaine must have gone through on that fateful night.

"How long do we have until they arrive?" Henry darted his eyes at Elaine, though they quickly returned to the horizon. That invisible line, where the ocean kissed the sky, really was quite remarkable.

"A week. Maybe two."

Henry looked off, calculating in his head, pondering how long it would take him to plan their escape.

"I can have the boat ready in a week. We could prepare food and gather what you would like to take back with us to New York," Henry proposed.

"I don't want to go back to New York," Elaine bluntly stated.

"Well," Henry reasoned, confused by her contradictions. "We could voyage to London. I've traveled there before, and it's a lovely place, Elaine. I really think you'd like it." When she said nothing, Henry pondered deeper, determined to accommodate her, and ultimately, make her happy. "Or we could visit Paris," he suggested. "Which would you prefer?" Henry prompted.

Elaine finally took her eyes off the horizon, and set her sights on the water around her.

"No, Henry," she said, her voice escalating in volume and pitch. "I don't want to go to Paris, or London, or any other part of Europe."

Henry could feel her rational thought slipping away, and it made him anxious. When Elaine made her mind up, not even the slightest possibility remained that he could change it.

"Then where would you like to go?" Henry calmly asked.

Elaine granted him the pleasure of looking in her eyes and uttered, "Home."

When Elaine swam to shore and left Henry floating in the ocean by himself, he slapped his hands over the water in frustration. If Henry was sure of anything about Elaine, it was that she was just as wild as that black jungle cat she loved so much. Elaine could not be locked in a cage. She would go crazy, pacing and hissing, until someone broke the lock and let her out.

New York was the only home Henry had ever known. And while he had enjoyed nearly every minute of his time spent here with Elaine, an exotic goddess if he had ever seen one, he couldn't help feeling a certain amount of happiness at the prospect of returning home. New York was the only place he truly wanted to be, but he wouldn't go without Elaine in his arms.

The problem was, Elaine viewed the city as a steel cage, meant to trap and imprison her. The jungle was her home now, and New York would only feel like barbed wire, cutting into her flesh, her spirit, her soul. How could Henry ever return to New York with a woman as free and untamed as the evergreen vines twisting and tangling through the jungle? Elaine had adapted to the natural world, and Henry had no way of getting her back to the girl she had once been in the city.

Henry swam to shore with these worries on his mind, teasing and tantalizing him in the form of daydreams. For a moment, he had imagined a world where he could stroll the streets of Manhattan with Elaine Carmichael on his arm, showing her off at every ball, festival, and banquet. He would marry Elaine in front of friends and family, buy an estate in the country, and then treat her to the finer things in life with the hefty inheritance that he would undoubtedly receive from his father.

Louisa, his younger sister, would adore Elaine, so pleased to have an elder sister to visit. Surely, Louisa would come by the house often, especially when they began to have children. Henry was exceedingly glad at the prospect himself, because he had never longed for a woman to bear him a family until Elaine had come into his life.

Henry would give her whatever she wanted in New York. Silk gowns. Satin sheets. Gossamer curtains. Velvet furniture. Diamond earrings. He could give her anything she had ever dreamed of back in New York. But Henry feared that he couldn't give her what she desired most in the whole world: a life here, in the jungle.

As Henry trudged into the shack and found Elaine crying in front of the table, he feared that he may never be able to make her happy.

"Let me be, Henry," Elaine sobbed, hearing his footsteps at her back.

"Elaine." Henry grabbed her shoulders and

turned her around to face him. "I can give you a splendid life in New York, my darling." He clasped her face in his hands, gently caressing the skin beneath her eyes with his thumbs.

"I don't want a life in New York," she moaned, tears streaming down her face.

"But I thought you said-"

"Yes! We have to leave, Henry. But I don't want to. I've never wanted to." She pushed his hands away from her face and moved to the other side of the table, her back to him.

Henry rested his hands on his hips and sighed. Pondering, he remembered all of her actions up until this point and considered the possibility that she may be less callous than he had once believed.

"Is this why you tried to make me leave? You knew the men were coming, so you wanted to send me away. Is that it?"

Elaine turned around and looked at him through blurry tears. "I wanted you to be safe," she cooed.

Henry moved past the table and shortened the distance between them. When he took her face in his hands, she pleasantly trembled. "I hate watching you cry," he whispered.

"Then don't watch."

Henry hummed to himself, and then forced her lips apart with his own. Elaine closed her eyes and marveled at the way their mouths became fixed on each other's, like a force of nature. When Henry dug his fingertips into her sides, she sighed aloud, glad to let him press her body against the wall.

Fearlessly exploring, Henry planted his lips beneath her ear, along her jawline, between the strap over her shoulder and her neck, under her chin, and across her chest. Awakened by the feel of her skin, Henry knelt down and grasped the skirt of her dress between his fingers. He kept his eyes on hers, green and burning bright, as he pushed the garment over her thighs, her stomach, and her breasts, before pulling it over her head.

Henry dropped the dress to the floor, while Elaine stood wanton and panting before him. Feeling as sultry and sensual as the goddess that she was, Elaine led Henry to their cot against the wall and pushed him down onto the bed. Henry lay on the flat of his back and held her in his arms, running his fingers through her long, black glorious locks. She leaned over his body and kissed him sweetly, wanting to show him how much he meant to her, how much she wanted him, how much she cared.

Henry traced the length of her bare back with his fingertips, moving his mouth with and against hers, until he grabbed her waist and pinned her beneath him. Rearing back, Henry quickly undressed, and then returned to Elaine, folding his hands with hers. The look in her evergreen eyes was so vulnerable, so naked, so innocent, that Henry stared down at her and smiled.

"I never knew how real life could be, until I

met you," Henry confessed.

Elaine curved her mouth into a pleasant grin, though the faintest glistening of teardrops in her eyes did not go unnoticed by Henry. Gentle and affectionate, Henry kissed all of Elaine's tears away and gave her every ounce of his love, because he had been living as a ghost without her in New York.

Elaine was fire and color and passion and excitement. All of the things that he had been lacking in his lonely world. She was the woman that all men dreamed of, that actresses in the theatre attempted to embody, and that fathers prayed their daughters would one day become.

Elaine was good. Elaine was strong. But most importantly, she was nearly impossible to find.

And as she lay beneath him, unraveling at his touch, Henry felt sure that Elaine was the kind of woman that, in his lifetime, he would never have the privilege of finding again.

## Chapter 18

**D**ays passed, and before long, Henry had fashioned a sturdy, reliable boat that he felt sure would transport them to New York safely. When Henry brought Elaine out of the shack to look at his carpentry, a strange influx of emotions spread across her face. Elaine knew how fitting the boat appeared, but with that observation also came the realization that Henry would wish to leave sooner, in case the pirates should arrive ahead of schedule.

"What do you think?" Henry motioned towards the boat, incredibly proud of the effort he had put forth to construct the watercraft in such a short amount of time.

"It's lovely, Henry," Elaine replied, biting her nails. She was terrified, because the plans that Henry had made were now becoming her reality.

"We should leave by morning."

"What?" Elaine gasped, her head spinning.

"Elaine," Henry scolded. "You said we needed

to leave this place. You said we had to leave the island."

"I know my own words, Henry."

"And?" Henry countered. "You refuse to listen to them. Is that what you're getting at?"

Elaine's face lit up as she looked over Henry's shoulder and watched Jade enter the jungle. Henry turned around and followed Elaine's gaze. When he saw the panther, he couldn't help but scowl.

"Jade?" Henry prodded. "You won't leave because of your stupid cat?"

Elaine struck her hand against the side of his face, as Henry tensed his jaw in response. The couple stood before one another glowering, gritting, smoldering. Henry gazed down at her from underneath his eyelashes, hot air blowing through his flaring nostrils.

"I thought I meant something to you, as well," Henry accused. "Jade is an animal, and she'll never care for you the way I do. It's in her nature, Elaine. She can't help it."

Elaine took a step closer, until their faces were nearly touching.

"Jade will protect me," Elaine upheld. "She's my guardian angel. She protected me from you."

Henry scoffed at the remark, curling his lip at Elaine. "And when have I ever harmed you?" He grabbed Elaine's wrist with one hand and pointed to her forearm with the other. "That creature left these marks," Henry argued, "and these marks." He opened his shirt and reminded her of the scars on his chest and abdomen. Elaine's eyes began to water, as she thought of what to say next.

"For the past five years, Jade has been the only family I've had."

Henry was surprised by how much those words stung. She had meant more to him than he ever could have imagined. He had never guessed that she hadn't felt the same. "And what am I?"

Elaine wrapped her hands around her elbows and slowly inched away from him.

"Go to New York, Henry. You have a family who loves you, who's been waiting for you. You have a home."

"But New York is your home too," Henry insisted.

"My mother and father were my home," Elaine murmured. "My sisters. My brother. And they're all gone. I've got no family waiting for me and nothing to go back to. You have everything and everyone hoping for your return." Elaine blinked a few tears away, fluttering her eyelashes in the process. "Why, I'll bet every young socialite in Manhattan will be expecting a visit from you. You'll have more beautiful girls knocking on your door than ever before. Because, out of all the men who left New York to voyage across the Atlantic, you'll be the only one who returned."

Henry clenched his jaw, holding back the tears that he felt brewing.

"My reasons for staying go beyond Jade, beyond New York, beyond this island. Those men will come, and I'd rather you not be here when they do."

Henry saw the tears in her eyes and noticed the heartbreaking way her lip was trembling. In that moment, Henry understood. The pirates had murdered her father, and now, all of these years later, Elaine had patiently waited until the time presented itself to avenge his death. Henry wanted to help her, hold her, protect her. But he could sense that avenging her father's death was something that Elaine wanted to do on her own.

"Elaine, I can wait with you. And we could go home to New York after it's all over. We can take all of that treasure with us too, back to America."

"Don't touch that treasure," Elaine snarled, gritting her teeth.

"Why?" Henry jerked his head in response.

"Because that treasure killed my father."

Henry caressed the tops of Elaine's arms with his hands and sighed. "Elaine, if you just come with me tomorrow, I promise, I'll build a beautiful life for us in New York. You'll be happy." He brushed his thumb along her jawline, coaxing her, persuading her, placating her. If only his gentle touch had been incentive enough.

"You have no idea how terribly I am going to miss you," Elaine admitted. She burst into tears, dreadful, choking sobs, and then ran off into the jungle. By the time Henry went after her, she had disappeared.

\* \* \*

Henry lay in Elaine's cot and buried his face in the sheets, inhaling her sweet, intoxicating scent. How Henry wished to bottle the fragrance and return to New York with it, so that he may always remember the way she had smelled.

Elaine had yet to return from the jungle, but Henry had left the makeshift door to the shack open anyway. He still carried the hope with him that she might change her mind, that she might leave with him tomorrow, that she might accept his invitation to a happy life in New York, after all.

As Henry lay there in the dark, he heard the filmy tapestry over the doorway rippling in the wind. Exhausted, he accepted the tough journey that awaited him in the morning and closed his eyes. But then Henry heard the sound of something rustle, so he looked back over his shoulder and found Elaine crying in the moonlight.

"I know that I have no right to ask it of you," she whimpered, moving from the doorway into the room. "And I know that you must be angry with me." Henry leaned forward and sat up on the edge of the bed. "But this is our last night together," she sobbed, "and-"

Henry rushed towards Elaine and pulled her into his arms, silencing her cries with his more than willing mouth. His hands danced along the length of her arms, as he caressed her smooth, supple skin with his fingertips. In seconds, Henry pulled Elaine's dress over her head and tossed it aside. She took his face in her hands and pulled him closer, until not even a sliver of space remained between their bare bodies. Desperately clinging to Elaine's tender frame, Henry kissed every inch of her soft golden skin, knowing very well that he may never feel it beneath his again.

As he weaved his fingers through her lustrous black locks, Henry cherished every sensation. The sound of her breathing. The sight of her figure. The touch of her lips. The taste of her skin. Pressing her body into the cot, Henry planted his knees along either side of her slender waist and lifted her back with his hands.

Elaine whimpered at the feel of his body against hers and sat up to wrap her arms around him, as their lips became fixed on each other's, molding and moving and coaxing. Breathless, Elaine held her mouth ajar, her teeth skimming over Henry's jawline, as she scraped her nails across the hard muscle of his back. Henry trailed kisses along the length of her neck, while she tilted her head back in ecstasy.

In time, their writhing bodies began to glisten beneath a sheen of passion and sweat. Henry clutched Elaine's arms with his hands and lay her back down on the cot, then blessed her lips with a final kiss of tender affection, sweet longing, and gentle adoration. Deep down, Henry knew that he would never discover a love like Elaine's again.

Resting her head against his chest, Elaine

spread her fingers out along his ribcage and listened to the hammering rhythm of Henry's heart. She cried quietly in the night, as the tears collected on his skin, gently flowing from her eyes. Henry was covered in salt water, an organic mixture of his sweat and her tears.

The couple had created their own ocean of pain, loss, and regret, though neither would stop the other from drowning in it. Without Elaine in his life, Henry had no desire to hold his head above water. Hers was the only oxygen he had ever needed to breathe.

When neither could sleep, Henry returned his lips to Elaine's, cherishing her, calming her, loving her. Precious time was all they had left, and Henry would sooner die than squander it.

By morning, Henry and Elaine had surrendered to exhaustion, so they slept through sunrise, until he stirred awake, just before dusk. Henry let go of Elaine's hand, rose from the cot they had shared, and then glanced back at her one last time. She looked peaceful as she slept, like a child who had never known the dreadful terrors of the jungle or sea.

Henry moved through the white tapestry that hung over the doorway and treaded across the sand with relief. He knew that he had no plans to leave.

## Chapter 19

**E**laine woke to find herself alone in a mess of tangled white sheets. Without hesitation, she rolled onto her stomach and buried herself in the scent of Henry that remained. Tears were all she wanted, but they wouldn't come. So Elaine lay in misery, until she heard someone outside.

Elaine's heart fluttered at the hope that she hadn't missed him. Unable to stand the suspense, Elaine hurriedly dressed, fled from the cot, ran across the sand, and found Henry at the shoreline, loading his boat with supplies. Her feet slowed as she drew near, but her breathing had grown unsteady, just the same.

"Hello, Henry," she crooned.

Henry looked over his shoulder and saw her twisting her fingers together out of uneasiness. Elaine stood there in that thin, dainty white dress. The first he had seen her in, the last he would see her in. She reminded him of an angel, a goddess, a royal, a saint. And yet, the paradise that he had found in her arms was drifting away, sinking beneath his feet like quicksand.

"You should have woken me," she softly declared, captivating Henry entirely. His eyes danced across every feature of her beautiful being. Her black hair, golden skin, pink lips, and green eyes. Those eyes had always reminded him of the jungle, because they were just as deep and full of dark secrets, tainted by nature and her deadly, unwavering hand in fate.

"I thought I'd let you sleep."

Henry turned his back to her and continued packing the boat with food and supplies for the journey ahead. When he was finished, Elaine felt as though she might faint. Her knees felt weak, and she could hardly hold on to the breath inside of her. Henry was finally leaving, and she couldn't reckon with the emotion. She thought she might drown in it.

"Oh, Henry," she cried, falling into his embrace. Henry held her in his arms and smelled her hair, wondering if she would think it strange of him to clip a lock to take with him and keep. Always.

"Elaine, please come with me," Henry begged. His fingers lay splayed across her cheeks, as he held her face in his hands.

"I can't," she painfully sobbed, her chest burning with anguish and remorse.

"Then I'll stay on the island with you."

"NO!" Elaine moaned.

She withdrew from him, and then shoved her hands into his chest, pushing him closer to the boat, farther away from her. Henry stood on the sand, with the ocean at his back, while Elaine stared him down in silence.

"I would rather die here tomorrow," he vowed, "than return to New York and live a hundred years, if you won't be living them with me."

Elaine let Henry's words fill her with warmth, as her chest sagged and heaved, matching her uneven breathing. The light in Henry's eyes was so raw, so honest, so pure, that she could hardly stand to look at him anymore.

"Go, Henry!" she commanded. "Just get in your boat and leave."

Henry took a step towards her, which only made Elaine retreat further. Pain lanced through his chest, because everything that he would ever need was right here before him. But happiness, as much as Henry would ever know of it, had been a brilliant, fleeting moment, like a flash of lightning across the ocean sky. And Henry had never expected that electric pulse between them to end so soon.

"Elaine, I can't go without you," Henry confessed. His brown eyes danced across her face, while Elaine kept quiet. "You're my whole world. I never knew life until I met you. How many times do I have to say it?"

"And how many times do I have to say it? You must leave this island!" she shouted, pointing towards the horizon. Henry narrowed his eyes, then relaxed his shoulders and stared at her. He could sense the fear she was feeling, because it radiated from her body like a beam of dark light.

"Have you cared for me at all since I've been on this island? Have you ever cared for me, Elaine?" Henry placed his hands on his hips, then nodded when she showed no intention of replying. He stroked his beard and chuckled, which finally elicited a response.

"Why would you say something like that to me?" Elaine's voice sounded small, like the air in her lungs was fading fast. Then Henry saw the tears in her eyes and moved close enough to wipe them away. When Elaine let him, he could hardly believe it. "After all this time, you truly believe that I don't care?" she sniffled, her long black locks falling in her face from the wind. Henry pushed them away with his hands, and then lifted her face before his very own. Her skin had never felt more soft.

"No," Henry muttered. "But you're having a difficult time believing it yourself." Elaine furrowed her beautiful black brows and pouted up at him in that childlike way he had always adored. "Please, Elaine," he begged. "Come home with me. There's nothing left for us here on the island."

"I *am* home," she claimed. "And I'd rather watch this place burn than leave it to those men."

Henry's face fell, as he dropped his hands from her cheeks. There was no use in attempting to convince Elaine. She couldn't be reckoned with. "What am I going to do without you?"

Elaine cleared her throat and smiled. "Remember me."

That was all she asked of him.

"But I love you," he declared, letting the levy burst, as tears puddled in his eyes.

Elaine closed the distance between them and pulled Henry into her arms. "And I love you, Henry. That's why I want you to go to New York. Your family loves you, and they need you."

Henry pulled away, holding her at arm's length, as he gazed into her eyes. "And what if I need you?"

Swallowing, Elaine held his gaze with her stunning green eyes, as mesmerizing to him as always. He would never look into another woman's eyes the same, because they wouldn't be Elaine's.

"If you truly love me, Henry, then you'll do as I've asked. You'll leave this island and never return."

Henry was angry now. This young island girl, the only to ever claim his heart, was ruining his only chance of happiness. The same happiness that she had stirred up within him. He couldn't bear it.

"If you loved me, you would have never asked me to go," Henry snarled.

Looking to the sea, Elaine bit the edge of her lip and whimpered. When her eyes returned to

Henry's, she could hardly look past her own tears. "You have given me more joy than you could ever imagine," she sobbed. "You say that I have given you life, that I have woken you up, Henry. But you are wrong!" Elaine balled her hands into fists and rubbed her tears away. "Until you came into my life, I was withering away. So cold. So hungry. So alone. You gave me everything I ever dreamed of, Henry." Elaine placed her head on his chest and relished the touch of his hands on her back. "I have treasured every moment with you, but I have to let you go."

"All right, my love," Henry consented. He caressed the skin of her bare arms, and then leaned back. From her countenance, he could see that this was what she truly wanted. So, to spare her tears, he relinquished his own wishes and replaced them with hers. "Have I at least earned a farewell kiss?" He grinned, tucking a loose strand of hair behind her ear.

Elaine looked up at him and sighed. "It would be too painful."

For some peculiar reason, Elaine's reaction made Henry laugh harder than he had in a long time. Elaine fluttered her eyelashes at him, as startled as she was perplexed. Then Henry took her face in his hands and uttered, "Good."

His mouth met hers with familiarity, tears, and heartbreak. Elaine held her hand up at first, as if she were prepared to fight him off. But then the kiss deepened, and she wanted nothing more than to feel his arms around her.

Elaine braided her fingers through Henry's dark brown tresses, letting the electricity seep into her skin. Surely, she would never be nestled in the arms of a man again. But that made her last moment with Henry, and the previous night, all the more valuable.

When Henry lifted his lips from hers, Elaine was caught in a trance, and by the time, she looked up, he had already climbed into his hand-made watercraft and sailed away. Wiping the last tears from her eyes, Elaine looked down to find Jade resting in the sand by her side. She watched that small boat move across the ocean, as the sun sank deeper into the skyline. And when the image of Henry became a drifting speck, she placed her hand over her stomach, where the life of his child was forming inside her.

# Chapter 20

**H**enry dipped the wooden oar that he had fashioned from the palm trees into the ocean, as the horizon pushed outward. Then, when the sun disappeared and a glow of green flashed across the fine line, where the sea kissed the sky, Henry put the oar aside, content to drift and float.

Elaine may have believed that she had Henry's best interest at heart. But he had no intention of living in a world where she was not. And when the lingering light of day finally faded, he would paddle back to shore and surprise Elaine beneath the moonlight. They would return to her cot and resume the passions of the previous night, until neither of them could breathe without the other.

Just as dusk faded into twilight, Henry widened his eyes in terror, for his plans were now inextricably foiled. Up ahead, on the horizon, appeared a bounteous ship with red sails, and it was headed towards the island.

\* \* \*

Elaine lay in her cot, consumed by grief, overwhelmed with tears, full of regret. As she sobbed quietly, mourning the loss of Henry, guilt swept through her like an ocean storm. How could she let Henry leave without telling him that she was carrying his child?

How cruel, how unspeakable, how selfish of her to do such a thing. But Elaine couldn't help feeling obligated to send Henry away in his ignorance. She had already decided that those men would pay for what they had done to her father, when she was no more than sixteen, stranded alone in what first appeared to be paradise, with small young Jade as her sole source of comfort.

Henry was gone. Henry was out of her life. And it had all been her doing. Now, there was nothing left to do but wait.

Drying her eyes, Elaine rose from the cot and brushed whatever traces of tears were left from her dress. Jade approached the entrance to the shack and growled, a primal warning that had not left her mouth since Henry washed ashore. Looking out the window, Elaine watched the large ship with red sails reach the shoreline.

Prepared as always, Elaine rushed over to the cabinet and retrieved a silver dagger, her father's dagger, the dagger that she would plunge into the heart of his murderer. Lifting the skirt of her dress, Elaine strapped the blade to her thigh, just above her knee, then secured the weapon in place, before concealing it beneath her clothing.

When Jade roared again, Elaine stepped out of the shack and watched the three men coming towards her. Their ship floated just past the shoreline, a haunting backdrop that sat like a mountain of intimidation behind them.

Though she knew none of their names, Elaine recognized the one in the middle first. He was blonde, tan, tall, the tallest, in fact. But he was also the man who she had watched kill her father.

The other two looked more alike: black hair, brown eyes, brand marks wrapping around either of their forearms. She immediately remembered thinking that they must have been brothers.

Elaine offered an innocent smile from her distance, but before she could meet them in the sand, Jade ran past her and pounced on top of the blonde one. In the moment it took Elaine to realize what Jade had done, she thought that she must have intuitively sensed that he had been the one to murder her father.

"Jade!" Elaine raced towards her, surprised, but also terrified by how the other men might react.

The big cat's victim lay beneath her, on the flat of his back, as the tide barely reached the ends of his shoulder-length hair. Jade struck her claws against the side of his face and hissed in a way that would make any grown man's blood curdle.

Elaine intended to call her back, but could not.

The man screamed and cried out, begging, much in the same way her father had that night. One of the other men, who was called Samson, rushed across the sand and picked up a piece of driftwood. Elaine failed to reach him in time, before he beat the panther across the nose with it. Then the other one, a man named Peter, pulled a length of chain from the pocket of his trousers and tossed it over and around Jade's neck.

"No!" Elaine screamed, her eyes widening in fear and panic.

Jade fought against the chain, rearing back, as she stood up on her hind legs. But she was restrained.

"She'll make a nice new coat for your girl. Huh, Judas?" the man holding Jade back said.

Elaine glanced down at the man on the ground, realizing that Judas must have been his name.

"Please," Elaine begged. "Don't hurt her."

Peter helped Judas off the ground, as Elaine took a weary step back in the sand. Judas stroked his fingers through his blond locks, pushing the disheveled pieces out of the way. Then he bent down and cupped his palm in the ocean, splashing water along the side of his face.

"Is she your pet?" Judas asked, his deep, raspy voice sending a jolt through Elaine's body.

"My pet?" Elaine stammered.

"Yes," Judas hissed. He stood up straight, slung his hair back, and then hovered before her.

"Your pet."

In such close proximity, Elaine observed how terrifyingly tall and muscular and threatening Judas looked. He let his arms dangle at his sides, as he clenched his hands into two great big fists. Elaine didn't want to be reminded of what he could do with them.

"I know where the treasure is," Elaine abruptly revealed.

Peter and Samson perked up immediately, their heads bobbing to the sky. But Judas remained unmoved.

"What treasure?" he tested. Elaine kept her head down, softly gazing at the sand. Impatient, Judas tugged her chin up with his thumb and forefinger and growled, "What treasure?"

"I'm sorry," Elaine crooned, glancing up at him from beneath her eyelashes. "I thought you knew."

Judas held her innocent gaze and narrowed his cobalt blue eyes in response. Without intention, his hand moved to the side of her face, and Elaine stilled.

"It's been ages since I've felt of a woman's skin," he confessed.

Judas brushed his thumb along Elaine's cheekbone, and then traced the edge of her jawline with his finger. When his hand dropped from her face, Elaine lowered her gaze and resumed breathing.

"So," Judas went on, amazed by the distraction

of her charms. "Tell us of this treasure, island girl."

Elaine's eyes flickered among the three men, then landed on Jade's. The big black cat stared at Elaine, then turned her head towards the jungle. Elaine knew their thoughts were the same.

"There is treasure on this island," she announced. "Rubies and diamonds and emeralds. The sheer gold would astound you." Elaine was looking at all of them, though, at the end of every sentence, her gaze always returned to Judas and lingered. "I don't know why it is here or who left it. But I'll show you where it is. Just leave Jade alone."

At first, the men stared at her in silence, which caused the skin above Elaine's upper lip to perspire. Finally, Judas burst into laughter and the other two followed suit. Elaine smiled in the smallest of ways, then tried not to flinch when Judas draped an arm over her shoulder.

"Very well," he granted. "You may have your cat, as you wish."

Judas smelled of Elaine's lustrous black hair, as Jade stepped towards them. Peter jerked back on the chain, and Jade protested with the bearing of her fangs.

"Samson," Judas called. "Go with her. We must learn of this so-called treasure."

Samson stepped forward and explored Elaine's figure with his eyes. She felt her stomach twisting into knots, even before she noticed the pistol hanging from his hip.

"Well," Judas urged, clapping his hands together. "Go on then."

Samson strode past them and headed towards the jungle. As Elaine turned on her heel, Judas stopped her with another question. "Why Jade?" he wondered, eyeing the beautiful black panther from where he stood.

"Her eyes," Elaine replied, watching Jade. "It's the color of her eyes."

Judas hummed to himself silently, then nodded. "I like it. Go on now. Show Samson the dear treasure, and I promise Jade will remain untouched."

Elaine's eyes darted to the dirty, scarred hand over his chest. When he extended it towards her, it was with a heavy heart that she shook it. Samson was waiting for her at the edge of the jungle, so Elaine pulled her hand out of Judas's rough, calloused grip and walked away.

"Why did you send Samson?" Peter asked, his fading voice still loud enough for Elaine to hear.

"On the ship, I saw a skiff in the distance," Judas explained. "There was a man on it, and he was much too close. He must have seen us, as well."

"Did you recognize him?"

"No. But he'll come to shore, and when he does, we'll be waiting."

Elaine's heart sank, as she joined Samson, just before the jungle. All the trouble she had created, just to spare the one she held most dear. And now, he would stumble directly into a trap, anyway.

Elaine had every intention of freeing Jade. But the only one she could think about was *Henry*.

# Chapter 21

Samson slapped green vines and foliage away with his forearm, as he and Elaine plunged deeper into the dark forest. The sun had fully set, with no remnants of the soft orange glow left. When Elaine looked up at the sky now, there was nothing more than a flat tapestry of black.

Reaching the lagoon, Elaine gestured to Samson with her hand and stepped into the pool of water. Samson followed suit and swam after her, gliding underneath the waterfall, until they both came up on the other side. He had yet to question Elaine's sense of direction, because he already knew where the treasure was. And as they entered the cave and traveled through intricate passages, Elaine's earlier instincts were confirmed.

Samson had taken this path before, but he, like Judas and Peter, had yet to believe that she had as well. When Elaine approached the old wooden door and pulled the key from her breast, Samson grabbed her wrist and glared at her. "Where did you get that?"

"I found it on the beach," Elaine whimpered. "It was in the sand."

Samson ripped the key out of her hand, breaking the chain of the necklace around her throat. Elaine cried out in anguish, as he opened the door and stepped inside, striding across the cool, bare floors. Consumed with shock, Elaine's eyes widened in bewilderment.

All of the treasure was gone.

Fuming, Samson stalked towards Elaine and slammed the door, locking them both inside. Elaine's back pressed into the wall, as he breathed down upon her, his dark eyes wild with fury. For the life of her, she could not understand how the treasure had seamlessly vanished.

"What have you done with it?" Samson sneered. "Answer me!"

"Nothing," Elaine moaned, "I swear."

Samson struck his hand against the side of her face and then released her, only so he could pace the floor. Tears streamed down Elaine's face, as she took a string of powerful, heaving gasps of air. Once again, all she could think about was Henry.

"Judas won't believe me," Samson assumed. "He'll think I moved it." Groaning aloud, he spotted a lonesome gold coin, the only piece of value left in the room, and kicked it across the floor. "However did you move such a lot?"

"I didn't move it," Elaine declared. "And I'm not lying."

Taking her by surprise, Samson strode across the floor and held out his hand. Elaine narrowed her eyes at him and swallowed, but reluctantly gave him her hand. He pulled her along with him, then walked to the center of the room. When he let her hand go, she did not understand.

"Turn around," he murmured. Elaine thought her heart might explode out of her chest, but she did as he said. "Keep turning," he coaxed, until Elaine had formed a complete circle. When she was facing him again, Samson grabbed her wrist and told her to stop.

"You may be dishonest," he supposed. "But aren't we all?" Samson smiled, revealing a pair of rotting yellow teeth. His stench was more than enough to send bile racing up the back of Elaine's throat.

Samson twirled a finger through one of Elaine's shiny black locks, then drew a line down her neck and over her collarbone. When his touch reached the edge of her breasts, Elaine batted his hand away. Samson's dark, shaggy mane jostled in response, because she had almost knocked him off his feet.

Livid, Samson wrapped his fingers around her throat and slammed her back against the wall. Elaine cried out in pain, especially when he forced the back of her head into the hard surface. Writhing, Elaine winced at the impact, her head throbbing in agony.

Samson lowered his face over hers and

muttered, "Perhaps there is some use for you after all."

Paralyzed, Elaine shook with fear as Samson knelt down before her, his hand sliding along her left leg. Samson kissed her calf and kissed her knee, his eyes wandering to what lay above them. He squeezed her thigh with his hand, and then stopped to gaze up at her.

"I haven't seen a creature like you in ages," he confessed.

Elaine remained perfectly still, as his eyes returned to the half of her body that rested below her waist.

In vain, he spoke to her body: "Father, forgive me, for I have sinned."

In a series of swift movements, Elaine lifted her dress, grabbed the dagger, and plunged it into the side of Samson's neck. Within seconds, he fell back and crumpled onto the floor, his mouth opening and closing, as he desperately searched for air.

Samson pulled the blade from the wide slit it had formed in his neck, then dropped it onto the floor. Blood drained from his body like a pierced fish, until he stopped moving and sputtering altogether.

Breathless, Elaine carefully stepped around Samson's body and knelt down to retrieve the key from his pocket and her dagger from the floor. Once she did, Elaine bolted across the room and unlocked the door. When she turned back,

Samson's body still lay bloody and lifeless on the ground.

Returning to the body, Elaine grabbed his hands and dragged him across the floor, despite his heavy weight. Once she reached the doorway, Elaine pulled Samson out of the room, and then pushed him off the edge, until he fell into the water down below. She watched him sink, until she couldn't bear to watch any longer.

With her blood still pulsing, Elaine locked the door to the former treasure room, and then dropped the key into the water. There was no need to keep it now. Besides, Elaine had no desire of ever returning to the cave after tonight. All she could picture was Samson's dead body, drifting to the bottom.

Worried that Judas and Peter would come looking, Elaine dove into the water and swam with speed and agility, desperate to be out of the cave. But something grabbed her leg, pulling her back, as Elaine let out a startled scream. She turned her head to find Samson tugging at her heel, still struggling to survive, despite the open wound in his neck.

Elaine snatched the dagger from beneath her dress and stabbed the other side of Samson's neck. Then she pulled the blade out and stabbed him three times in the chest, for good measure, until the weak grip around her leg loosened and he descended deeper into the water.

Starved of oxygen, Elaine returned the dagger

to its sheath and swam underwater for what seemed like an eternity, until she finally surfaced in the lagoon. Her lungs burned as she came up for air, choking and coughing and gasping. Elaine pulled herself out of the lagoon and collapsed onto the ground, down on her knees, as she wept into her hands. But she failed to let her tears consume her for long, always looking over her shoulder to see who may be quietly approaching in the jungle.

Rising to her feet, Elaine cleaned herself off with water from the lagoon, then washed off the blood from her dagger. Despite the darkness, Elaine worried that Judas and Peter would notice the blood stains on her dress. The pale white fabric provided such a striking contrast, that Samson's blood would be hard to miss. So, Elaine tossed water onto her dress, to lessen the appearance of the stains, and then stood to leave. As she turned around and gazed up at the sky, Elaine could not help but take off running, at the sight of smoke in the distance.

## Chapter 22

**H**enry paddled furiously ahead, his greatest enemy the harsh waves beneath him. His boat had to be strong enough. His boat had to be fast enough. Because Henry had to reach the island. He had to get to Elaine. He had to save her before they took her from him forever.

Struggling, Henry gritted his teeth together and groaned. His muscles couldn't take anymore pushing and pulling. His back was sore, and his arms were burning.

But Henry couldn't stop.

He wouldn't stop.

Only death would keep him from reaching Elaine. And Henry felt that his will to live was so strong that the ominous threat was not even a worry anymore.

Up ahead, Henry saw firelight on the beach, in the exact place where Elaine had shared her fish with him, when he had been no more than a stranger. He remembered the first day he had washed ashore on the island, so astonished to have found paradise instead of death. He felt the scars on his chest and abdomen, where Jade had clawed at him and made him bleed.

Looking back, Henry decided that it had all been worth it. The fear. The blood. The tension. The arguments. The distance. The frustration. The confusion. The panther. The poison. The quicksand. The berries. The boat. Even that cat, Jade.

Everything had been worth just a moment in Elaine's arms, the scent of her hair, the warmth of her cheeks, the sound of her voice, the feel of her body tightly wrapped around his.

He couldn't turn back now. He couldn't stop to rest, or quell the painful burning in his arms. All he could do was move forward, closer to Elaine, closer to her arms, closer to home.

Even as the tide calmed, Henry worried that he was too late, that he wouldn't make it in time, that Elaine was already dead. But Henry was too inextricably bonded to Elaine. Heart, body, and soul.

Wouldn't he know if she had breathed her last breath?

Wouldn't he be able to feel the loss of her all around him?

Wouldn't he sense that his entire world had ended?

Shaking his head, Henry forced those thoughts into the deepest crevices of his mind. That is, until he heard Elaine's piercing scream, echoing, traveling, carrying out across the ocean.

# Chapter 23

When Elaine returned to the beach, her heart rippled with anger and sadness. In her time away, Judas and Peter had placed a large metal cage on the stretch of sand that stood between the shack and the jungle. They had also locked Jade inside of it.

Moaning, Elaine stood in front of the cage and stuck her hand through one of the square holes, reaching out for Jade. The panther's eyes lit up at the sight of Elaine, as she lifted her head for Elaine to pet. But before the two could make contact, Judas locked his arms around Elaine's stomach and jerked her away.

Elaine screamed at the top of her lungs, causing Judas's ears to ring until he threw her onto the sand, in front of the fire. She cried aloud as her nails dug into the ground. And when Judas sat down to share a bottle of rum with Peter, Elaine took a clump of sand in her palm and pitched it at his face.

Blinded by the sand, Judas returned the rum to Peter, and then rubbed the sand from his face. When he could see again, Judas snatched Elaine up off the ground and twisted her elbow every step of the way, until they reached the cage.

"NO!" Elaine shrieked, realizing his malevolent intentions. "NOOOOOO!"

Judas opened the door to the cage and forced her inside, imprisoning her with Jade. With a sinister smirk, he slipped the key in his pocket, and then leaned against the metal bars.

"You think it's your friend," Judas teased. "But when it gets hungry, you'll see just how friendly it can be."

"Jade would never hurt me," Elaine countered, talking through the bars.

Judas pressed his head against the bars to intimidate her. "She's an animal, island girl. I can assure you that she is going to get very hungry."

"You could never understand it," Elaine insisted, wrapping her fingers around the metal bars to look deeper into his eyes.

Judas smiled. "She's a predator. It's in her nature. And every fiber of her being will tell her to eat you. We're going to watch, and when she's done, we'll kill her, skin her, and make a shiny new coat with it."

Elaine slammed her palms into the metal bars before his face. But Judas merely chuckled, looking on in delight, as Elaine begged to be let free. He strolled back over to the fire and joined

Peter.

When the rum ran dry, Peter opened the hidden hatch in the sand and climbed down below for another bottle. Judas turned around in the sand to face Elaine and Jade, then pulled his knees into his chest and sighed. "Where's Samson?" he wondered.

"In the cave," she replied, yelling so he could hear her, despite the distance between them.

"Even now?"

"Yes, he's collecting the treasure to put on the ship."

Peter surfaced without troubling himself enough to close the hatch in the sand. He stumbled back over to Judas, in front of the fire, holding a bottle of rum for each of them. Judas and Peter popped the corks, clinked bottles, and then swallowed all that they could in one gulp.

Utterly defeated, Elaine stared through the metal bars, watching Judas and Peter strive for intoxication, while Jade began pacing the length of the cage.

## Chapter 24

W hen Henry's boat made contact with the sand, he leapt out and pulled the skiff out of the water. Running backwards, he dragged the watercraft up to the base of a palm tree and ducked down behind the shack. As he crept around the perimeter of the shack, Henry listened to the voices of Judas and Peter. Both men came into view, their backs turned to Henry, as they chuckled and drank in front of the fire.

Crouching down low, Henry peered around the edge of the shack and spotted Elaine seated in the cage, with her back against the metal bars. Judas stood up from the fire and wobbled over to the cage, taunting Elaine with his drunken antics. Jade lay silently beside Elaine, her chin resting on a pair of crossed front paws.

"I see you, island girl," Judas whispered, walking around the cage until he was beside her. "You and your jungle cat."

Elaine sat with her legs sprawled out, her arms

folded across her chest. Henry watched from the edge of the shack, careful not to reveal his hiding place.

"Come here," Judas ordered, commanding Elaine to move closer, but she would not move. "Look at me!"

Judas stuck his hands through the bars and pulled Elaine's hair, controlling the direction of her head, so she was forced to look back at him. Immediately standing up on all fours, Jade hissed, bearing her slimy white fangs before she charged the metal bars in front of Judas. With a wicked smirk, he stepped away from the cage and fell back on the sand.

Jade leaned into the bars and stood up on her hind legs, clawing and growling and scratching, as she reached her vengeful paw through an open slit of air in the cage.

Chuckling darkly, Judas stood up and, much to the relief of Jade and Elaine, walked off until he had disappeared into the jungle. Jade backed away from the bars and returned her front paws to the ground. Elaine relaxed her body and breathed a sigh of relief, closing her eyes for only a moment. When she opened them, Elaine found Jade, nudging the top of her head into Elaine's palm. She smiled down at the familiar gesture and stroked Jade's beautiful fur coat, rubbing the panther behind her ears and under her chin. Jade purred in response, placing her head in Elaine's lap and kneading her paws with delight.

Peter fell asleep in front of the fire, loudly snoring, to the amusement of Elaine. Spotting an opportune moment, Henry came out from behind the shack and crept his way towards the resting drunk. When Elaine saw him, her eyes widened in astonishment, and she froze in place, believing that his figure was no more than an illusion.

Henry held a finger to his lips to silence the look of surprise on Elaine's face. She held her breath as he crept closer, his feet sinking into the sand with each step. Once he neared the fire, Henry studied Peter's slouching figure, listening to his heavy breathing. Slowly and carefully, Henry approached the cage and glanced down at Elaine.

"Henry," she gasped, standing up and rushing to the front of the cage. "I thought you were gone forever." Elaine wrapped her hand around one of the metal bars and gazed into his eyes with adoration. "One of the men saw you, Henry. They've known you were coming. I just didn't believe it."

Feeling as though he were being watched, Henry turned his head to look back over his shoulder, but Peter had yet to move.

"Judas will return soon," Elaine relayed. "You have to let us out of here, Henry. Quick."

"Judas?" Henry eyed the lock on the cage and tried to force it open.

"The one who killed my father," Elaine clarified. "He has the key. Please, Henry. Hurry."

His eyes flickered in fear, as he took off

running and only came to a stop when he reached the skiff. A box of tools sat in the bottom of the boat, the same tools that Henry had used to construct it. Frantic, he flipped the lid open and grabbed a hammer. Then he ran back across the sand with the weapon in tow and motioned for Elaine to step back. When she did, Henry lifted the hammer over his shoulder and brought it down against the lock. Despite the impact, Elaine and Jade were still trapped inside.

"Hurry, Henry. Hurry," Elaine pleaded, her voice low and anxious.

Using a tremendous amount of force, Henry slammed the end of the hammer into the lock again. But, in the end, it took three sharp blows for him to finally break the lock.

Elaine and Jade pressed their faces against the metal bars, until Henry opened the door to the cage and set them free. The first stepped across the sand and leapt into Henry's arms, while the second bolted out of sight, headed straight towards the jungle.

"Henry," Elaine cried, wrapping her arms around his neck. "I'm so sorry I told you to go. I was wrong. Will you ever forgive me?"

"Yes, my darling." Henry pulled Elaine into his embrace and smelled of her hair. "Have they hurt you?"

Henry held Elaine at arm's length and noticed the mark across the side of her face, where Samson had struck her. Brushing his thumb across her cheek, Henry stiffened at the sight of her wincing. One of these men had hurt her, and Henry wanted nothing more than to watch him suffer.

"Henry," Elaine murmured, her green eyes steadily fixed on what lay beyond his shoulder. One subtle click made Henry freeze in place, as he turned around to find Peter aiming a pistol at them, cocked and ready to fire.

Elaine knelt down to collect the broken lock in her hand, causing Peter to turn the pistol on her. When she rose from the ground, Peter gladly took the lock from her. And when his gaze shifted to the fractured metal, Elaine threw a heap of sand in his face.

While Peter coughed and groaned, he stumbled backwards and tripped over his own bottle of rum. The beverage leaked out, pooling around the fire, until flames tore across the trail the rum had made. By the time Peter looked up, Henry and Elaine were gone.

## Chapter 25

Entering the jungle, Henry and Elaine sought cover behind a robust gathering of palm fronds and watched Peter discover their absence. As he slapped the dusty sand from his face, Peter held the gun in the air and fired. Then his focus centered on the jungle, where he aimed the pistol, even though Henry and Elaine remained well hidden.

They ducked down low, hearing the bullet race over their heads, as Henry shielded Elaine's body with his own. Peter trudged closer, inherently sensing their presence in the jungle. So Henry grabbed Elaine's hand and looked at her.

"Go find Jade," Henry instructed, squeezing her palm at the sound of another flying bullet.

"What?" Elaine resisted.

"I'll distract him," Henry explained. "Now, go find Jade."

Elaine held Henry's eyes with her own, unable to move, unable to decide.

"Go!"

In the end, the choice was not Elaine's to make. Henry shoved her away from him, barking for her to disappear into the darkest depths of the jungle, until she finally did. Immediately regretting the separation, Henry followed her silhouette with his eyes, until it was nothing more than a memory.

Disgruntled, Henry returned his focus to Peter, as the drunken pirate sashayed to and fro. The spreading fire caught Henry's eyes, as he watched an orange-red blaze consume a stray bottle of rum in the sand. Peter noticed the growing flames and turned his back to the jungle.

Henry took advantage of the moment and jumped over the hedge of fronds, tackling Peter to the ground. The pistol turned loose from his hand, as both men struggled to reach it first. Peter punched Henry in the jaw, as his other hand traveled backwards, crawling towards the gun.

When Peter set the edge of his fingertips on the handle, Henry grabbed the man's shoulders and slammed his body into the ground. But Peter had garnered a decent grip on the pistol, as the weapon slid nicely into the palm of his hand.

Widening his eyes, Henry grabbed Peter's arm and jostled it so violently, that the pistol slipped out of his hand, just as easily as it had slid into it. Peter punched Henry again, then kicked him in the stomach, but Henry fought back like the savage he had become the day he slaughtered that panther in the jungle.

With every brutal blow, he only thought of Elaine, assuming that Peter had been the one to strike her. And when Peter's face was so unrecognizably marred with hot blood and swelling flesh, Henry rose to his feet and collected the pistol from the ground.

Peter lay helplessly in the sand, overpowered by Henry's tenacious will to live. As Henry stepped closer, surveying Peter's trembling body from where he stood, an icy coldness filled his body. So much so, that the feeling stung his skin from the inside out. Holding his chin taut, Henry glared down at Peter and cocked the gun.

"No!" Peter screamed, blood guzzling from his mouth and staining his teeth. "Please," he mumbled, "I beg of you, sir. Please, don't."

Henry exhaled a stream of hot air through his nostrils and pulled the trigger. The bullet pierced through the top of Peter's skull and silenced him forever. Shaking, Henry dropped the empty pistol to the ground and clenched his teeth to withhold the tears forming in his eyes.

His mind immediately flashed to images of Charles. A memory of one of their many fishing trips. Charles had caught the last fish of the day, a three hundred-pound marlin to be exact. Quite an achievement for twenty-seven-year-old Charles at the time. But Henry had released the hook from its mouth and tossed it back into the sea.

"Henry Rochester! I will drown you in these waters," Charles threatened, shoving Henry's arm.

"What on earth possessed you to do such a thing?" Charles shook his head and glared at Henry. He couldn't understand.

"Haven't we caught enough fish today, Charles?" Henry glanced up at him seriously, while the wind picked up, sending a gentle breeze through his hair.

"No!" Charles demanded. "Have you learned nothing about fishing, boy?"

Charles rose and walked across the boat to collect a bottle of brandy. When he returned to Henry and sat back down, the glass rim was firmly attached to his lips. Henry placed his hands on Charles's shoulder and sighed with regret.

"I'm sorry, Charlie," he muttered. "That was very wrong of me. I just couldn't bear to watch one more creature die for sheer sport."

Charles pulled back on the bottle, and then handed it to Henry. "I fear I will never understand you, dear friend," he confessed. Henry drank from the bottle, then let Charles take it from him.

"I'm sorry," Henry repeated.

"Ah," Charles chuckled, only talking between swigs, "wasn't that big... I'll find another."

But he never would.

That same night, in the billiard room of the Rochester Mansion, Charles pondered over that three hundred-pound marlin. Henry lined up his cue stick and aimed to shoot the eight ball into the far left pocket, but landed another solid instead. As Charles went on jabbering, Henry set his sights on the two solids that remained on the green felt of the table.

"It really is quite remarkable, you know?" Charles claimed.

"What is?" Henry struck his cue against the white ball, but it merely tapped the one he had intended to sink.

"And it's got me thinking," Charles meandered, sipping out of his brandy glass with one hand, while his cue stick stood upright in the other.

"Are you going to stand there or take part in the game?" Henry grumbled.

"Fine," Charles consented, setting his glass on the edge of the table. He leaned over, eyeing the remaining balls, and lined his cue stick up accordingly.

"I'm much obliged," Henry quipped.

"You see, Henry, my young friend. You haven't lived enough years to understand me, but I am quite logical," Charles informed, closing one eye as he took aim.

"I'm sure I don't know what you mean," Henry rebutted, much to the amusement of Charles.

"Today, on the boat." Charles shot the cue stick forward, and the eight ball landed in the far left pocket with a resounding thud. "What if I had been that fish?"

Henry stood with his mouth agape, disappointed that he had lost the game. Charles returned the cue stick that he had played with to its case, then strode past Henry.

"You haven't answered me, young friend," Charles prodded.

Henry grinned, shaking his head. "I believe you've had far too much brandy this evening, Charlie."

"Answer me," Charles demanded, surprising Henry. "What if I had been that fish?"

"I told you before, Charlie," Henry declared. "I was wrong, and it was not my place. After all, it's only murder when they're human."

"Ah," Charles clicked his teeth together and smiled, pointing a finger at Henry. "But is it?" Charles glanced at Henry, then turned away and walked out the door.

Even now, Henry had yet to understand what Charles had said all those years ago. Had he meant that taking the life of an animal was the same kind of murder as taking the life of a human? Or, that in some cases, killing a man could be considered something other than murder?

Henry shook the thought from his head and blinked, as if he were seeing everything before his eyes for the very first time. The blazing trail of fire cut across the sand and forged a path towards the shack. In disbelief, Henry stepped back, as the closest palm tree lit up in flames.

## Chapter 26

Elaine slowly slunk through the forest, searching for Jade in the night. When she heard creatures rustling the bushes, Elaine removed the dagger from the sheath at her thigh and clutched it in her hand. But, instead of the animals she had anticipated, Judas came out of hiding and stalked towards her.

"You've killed Samson," he said, not waiting for her to confirm the truth. "I needn't ask why. Let me take care of Peter, and we'll divide the treasure between us." He took a step closer and a twig snapped beneath his boot. "Equal shares," he mused. "Equal halves, I promise."

"I have no desire for treasure, Judas. You may keep it all, and I'll make no complaint."

"Am I to believe such a lie?" Judas moved near her and snickered, his blonde hair illuminated by the shadows cast overhead. "The treasure is gone, and I know you have taken it. You have moved it. Tell me where."

"I found your maps!" Elaine revealed, raising the blade at him in defense.

"What?" Judas croaked.

"I found all of it," Elaine continued. "I found your maps, your calendars. And I know when you return. I know that you come back here, to this very island, every five years."

"How?" Judas appeared still, though his cobalt blue eyes were racing, searching for answers in the darkness.

"You killed a man here. Five years ago. On this very island!" Elaine pointed the edge of the blade towards him, her lips trembling at the memory of that dreadful night. "You killed my father."

Judas furrowed his brow, gazing over her with confusion. He turned his head to the side and studied the landscape surrounding him. The jungle no longer looked the same.

"I watched you!" Elaine cried. "I watched you kill him!"

"I'm very sorry," Judas whispered. "Please, forgive me." He reached his hand out towards her and missed the dagger. "I never intended for him to be killed."

Elaine gritted her teeth together and snarled, "Yes, you did."

Shrouded with anger, Elaine brought her fist to his face, and then kicked him in the stomach. Judas lurched forward, as Elaine lifted her foot in the air, her ankle connecting with his ear. Then she kicked him in the chest, and he fell to the flat of his back.

Climbing on top of him, Elaine pressed the cool, sharp metal of the blade to his throat.

"Just tell me," she whimpered. "Tell me why you hurt him. Tell me why you murdered him."

Though it was a lie, Judas could sense her weak spots, so he glanced up, into her eyes and said, "Because I knew you would be watching."

Squeezing Elaine's wrist, Judas pushed the blade away from his throat and pinned her to the ground beneath him. Elaine shrieked in terror, as he held the blade over the pulse point in her neck. Before he could cut into her throat, Jade leapt across the air and pounced on top of him.

Elaine sat up, quivering with fear, as Jade dug her claws into Judas's chest and growled in his face. But a treacherous gleam caught the corner of Elaine's eye, as she saw the dagger still firmly situated in his grip.

"NO!" Elaine wailed, but it was no use.

Judas plunged the dagger into Jade's heart, as the panther growled in anguish. He slipped out from Jade's hold, while Elaine ran to Jade, fell to her knees, and wept.

In a moment of vengeance, Elaine ripped the blade from Jade's heart and drove it into Judas's. He yelled out in tortured affliction, so paralyzed with shock, that he made no attempt to defend himself when Elaine removed the dagger, and then forced it back into his chest.

Once Judas drew his last breath, Elaine shuddered at the sound of Jade's weakened breathing. She stroked the panther's soft ears and gazed into her evergreen eyes, so much like her own that they were a mirror. When Jade turned her head and gazed at Elaine, something passed between the two that could not be described. Some have called it the splitting of a shared soul, while others merely refer to it as passing on.

"You were the only friend I ever had," Elaine wept, placing her palm against Jade's bleeding heart.

The panther licked the back of Elaine's other hand, then purred aloud when Elaine began to pet her again. Like an act of sorcery, Jade opened her mouth, about to speak, and then all of the air that remained left her lungs with a final exhale.

Elaine moaned in agony, weeping into Jade's soft fur coat. She screamed when a pair of arms grabbed her, trying to pull her away from Jade. "No!" she cried in terror.

"I'm sorry, Elaine," Henry spoke. "But we must go. The island has caught fire."

With every bit of reluctance, Elaine lifted her head to the sky and saw the smoke overhead. "I can't," she protested. Then, turning her focus to Henry, she finished, saying, "I can't leave her."

Elaine gazed down at her beloved friend, her guardian, her angel. She would give her a proper burial and let her body rest by the place where wild jasmine grew. The jungle was the only place either of them was ever destined to be.

Jade's tongue hung lifelessly from her mouth, her eyes staring into Elaine's. Still weeping, Elaine continued to pet Jade and attempt to console her, even though Henry was well aware that no consoling could bring that cat back from the dead.

Watching the smoke rise in the distance, Henry realized what he had to do. Though he knew Elaine would hate him for it, Henry pulled her away from the panther and dragged her, kicking and screaming, through the jungle.

Elaine put up a good fight, her piercing cries enough to make anyone's heart race. Eventually, he had no choice but to throw her over his shoulder and carry her the rest of the way. Once they reached the sand, Henry set Elaine on her feet, assuming that she would be too tired to run away from him. But when she did, it was all in vain, for Henry slung her back over his shoulder and continued onward.

"I hate you!" she screamed. "I wish you had never come! I wish you had died in the ocean with all of the others! I wish that storm had eaten you alive!"

Henry flexed his muscles, as Elaine beat her fists against his back. While her words stung, Henry knew that Elaine loved him, so he let her lose her wits for the time being. In a way, he could understand how Elaine felt about the death of her feline companion. It reminded him of how he felt about losing Charlie.

After dodging the fire, Henry grabbed what he could from the skiff, while still balancing Elaine's body over his shoulder. Then, he walked out into the sea and boarded the ship with red sails. He deposited Elaine on a cot below deck and locked the door behind him.

Henry felt bad about confining Elaine, especially at a time like this. But he didn't trust her judgment at present. She was just as likely to jump off the ship and drown as she was to toss Henry overboard. Moving forward, he remembered what he had learned during his brief voyage at sea and prayed that he would have the good fortune to avoid any possible storms.

After more hell than most living creatures could imagine, Henry and Elaine were finally going home.

## Chapter 27

Needing to rest, Henry anchored the ship and silently crept down the staircase, until he was below deck. The sound of Elaine crying sent lancing pain through his chest, as he strode towards the door that he had locked her behind. Once Henry opened it and stepped inside, he found Elaine sprawled out on the cot, her face in her hands. Taking a deep breath, Henry touched her shoulder and hoped for forgiveness.

"Elaine," Henry dared to say, fearing her eternal wrath. She ignored him at first, staring plainly at the wall before her. But then she sat up in the cot, looked back at him, and fell into his arms.

Henry gently consoled the woman he loved, relieved to have her head on his shoulder again. Wanting to ease her spirits, Henry traced patterns over her back with his hands and whispered in her ear until her tears lessened. When Elaine pulled away to gaze into his eyes, Henry pushed her hair out of her face and brushed his thumb along the length of her cheekbone, her jawline, her lips, as he had a thousand times before.

"I found Jade in the forest a few days before Father died," Elaine revealed, her voice trembling. "Something must have killed her mother, because Jade led me to the body. There was blood, and flies had begun to swarm. I don't know what happened, but Jade had no one. And a few days later, neither did I."

Holding her gaze, Henry trailed his fingers along the length of Elaine's neck and listened.

"Jade was my family, Henry," she sobbed. "My friend. Until you arrived, she was all I had."

"Well, I'm certain she's in a better place." Henry flicked his eyes to the floor, then back to Elaine's.

"Yes," Elaine agreed, surprised by his altered view of the afterlife.

"Jade loved you, Elaine," Henry admitted. "I never understood it, but I do now. She loved you as if you were her own mother. And you loved her in your own way, like a daughter. I should have been kinder to her."

"No," Elaine protested, planting her hand against Henry's cheek. "We had a beautiful life in the jungle, Henry. We all did. And Jade may be gone now, but I still have you."

Henry tilted his head to the side and placed his hand over hers. Unable to withhold her recurring emotions, Elaine lowered her head into Henry's chest and began to weep again. Aligning her pain with his own, Henry cradled Elaine in his arms and stroked his fingers through her glossy black locks.

Elaine welcomed Henry's tight embrace, as she listened to the steady, rhythmic beating of his heart. Her mind flashed through the evening past, though she tried to keep the dark thoughts at bay. Those men were dead now, and they had paid, particularly Judas, for what they had done to her father all those years ago. But there was no gratification, as she had anticipated and longed for. Instead, Elaine felt empty.

"I killed a man tonight," Henry murmured, his voice weak and full of sadness.

Lowering her eyes, Elaine reeled back and held Henry at arm's length. When he wouldn't meet her eyes, she tucked his dark tresses behind his ear and brushed her palm against the side of his face.

"I've never killed anyone before." Henry withdrew from Elaine and held his head in his hands, nervously weaving his fingers through his hair. In time, he would surely lose the ability to breathe, with the presence of this sickening feeling that had formed in the pit of his stomach. How did men in the militia reckon with this... this *darkness*?

"Henry, you had no choice," Elaine reasoned. "We had no choice."

"Did we?" Henry stared into her eyes with

languid sorrow.

"They would have killed us, Henry, and thought nothing of it."

"Maybe so..." Henry drifted off, lost in reality.

He had killed. Did that make him a *killer*? A *murderer*?

"No, Henry." Elaine shook her head. "I watched Father die, and they merely laughed."

"Elaine," Henry said.

"They deserved to die."

"Is that what death is?" Henry raised his voice. "Something to deserve? Something to be earned?"

"I don't know!" Elaine shouted, as her body began to quiver again.

Henry fell silent, letting his eyes drop down to the floor. All he wanted was to float out here forever, aimlessly drifting at sea, until he could no longer make out the faintest image of Peter's face. But Henry had to take Elaine home and build the life he had promised her in New York. He would make things right again.

"I'm going to have a baby," Elaine whispered, offering no warning beforehand.

Henry stiffened, his entire body freezing in place, like the Atlantic had swallowed him up whole in the middle of winter. But then a sweltering heat spread throughout his body, full of anger and thrill and fear. He could hardly swallow, for his mouth had gone completely dry.

"How long have you known?" Henry kneaded his hands together, burying one fist inside the palm of the other. His eyes shifted, racing across the floor, until he levelled them at Elaine.

"One week," she quietly replied.

"One week?" Henry rose to his feet and tossed his arms in the air, pacing and grunting and sighing. "How could you keep this from me?"

"Henry, I wanted to tell you but-"

"No, you didn't, Elaine!" Henry pointed his finger at her, fuming. "I know you. If you want to do something badly enough, you will. If you had wanted to tell me, you would have."

Elaine hung her head and held on to the edge of the cot, desperately wanting to lie down and rest. But Henry was the father of her child, and she had betrayed him. If only he could see why.

"You let me go!" Henry motioned his arm into the shape of a wide arc. "You let me leave! How could you send me away without telling me that you were going to have a child? My child."

"Henry, I-"

"What if I hadn't come back? I had already planned to return, but you didn't know that." Henry shook his head and crossed his arms over his chest. He would have resented her, had she been anyone else.

"Henry, I'm sorry," Elaine muttered under her breath. "I was just trying to spare you from-"

"From what?" Henry interrupted. He knelt down before her and took her hands in his. "I don't want a life without you, Elaine. Don't you know how much you mean to me?"

Henry waited for an answer from Elaine, but received a few glistening teardrops instead. Feeling responsible, he captured her face in his hands and lovingly looked into her eyes. Whether a boy or girl, he hoped their child had those beautiful, exotic evergreen eyes. They were far more precious than his own.

Unable to resist her charms, Henry brought Elaine's mouth to his and closed his eyes in contentment. She uttered a sweet, yearning sigh in response, prompting Henry to demolish the wall of secrecy and distrust that had formed between them. As their lips met again, Henry pressed Elaine's body into the cot, where she tilted her head back in longing. Henry tasted the skin of her neck, smoothing his fingers down the length of her arms, as he felt her body warming beneath him.

Breaking physical contact, Henry hovered over Elaine and remained still until she opened her eyes. When she did, Henry's gaze shifted to Elaine's stomach, distracted by the realization of the small life growing inside her. Henry eyed Elaine warily, making his intentions clear. She lay motionless, catching her breath, with her open hand resting above her head. A small exhale of air passed through her parted lips, as she followed his line of sight, and then nodded.

Careful, Henry delicately laid his fingers on top of Elaine's belly, his palm pressing into the soft, cool fabric of her white dress. Elaine studied every facet of his face, anticipating the reaction that would surely follow. She had imagined this moment many times in her dreams, when Henry would gladly welcome the news of the fragile life they had created together, but Elaine had never known that it would feel like this.

With his hand against her stomach, Henry let out a long-winded sigh and chuckled. His gaze returned to Elaine's, and the side of his mouth turned up into a crooked smile. Before Elaine could respond, Henry's mouth found hers, and the two were clinging to each other like vines wrapped around a tree.

Elaine unraveled at the touch of his fingertips, because she had so implicitly believed that Henry was gone forever. And when he slid his hands beneath the hem of her dress and tugged it loose over her head, she could not resist the slight distance between them any longer.

Greedy and willing, Elaine unbuttoned Henry's shirt and pushed the fabric past his shoulders, so she could feel the hard planes of muscle beneath his skin. When her fingernails tore at his flesh, Henry groaned in response, but Elaine muted the sound by covering his mouth with her own. Henry toyed with the button of his trousers, then tossed them aside once he was free of his clothes. Impatient as ever, Elaine grasped Henry's arm and pulled him closer, until a lingering moan escaped from both of their mouths.

The ship swayed to the steady beating of the waves moving beneath them, but Henry and

Elaine were hardly listening to anything other than the sound of their own breathing. Elaine scraped her teeth against Henry's chin, as he buried his face into her neck, wholly consumed by her love. If anything, the pregnancy had only increased Henry's attraction towards Elaine, since she was carrying the life of his unborn child. Henry seized Elaine's lower lip with his mouth and tugged at her soft, supple skin. Even though the news was fresh, Henry had already begun to imagine what their grandchildren would look like.

# Chapter 28

Time passed, and before Henry knew it, the seasons had changed. His nautical knowledge may have been scarce, merely drawing upon the months he had spent aboard the ship with Charles and company, but Henry followed the maps, allowing the aid of a compass and telescope to guide him. Equally engaged, Elaine followed her instincts and showed Henry the way, relying on the wind and rain to lead them home.

The weather turned colder, once autumn slipped away and winter replaced it. But the couple remained fearless, determined to reach their destination, ready to be home, prepared to rejoin the civilized world.

The ship had been stocked with an enormous supply of food, and Henry had brought what he could from the skiff, so life at sea was less intolerable than it could have been. Oftentimes, Elaine became sick, though neither could be sure if it were the direct cause of the rippling ocean tide that jostled the boat at times, or the current condition of her body. Regardless, Elaine failed to complain of the nausea that periodically swept through her. She and Henry had cheated death so many times that it hardly seemed logical to criticize the second chance at life, which they had so mercifully been given.

On their last night at sea, Elaine searched for food among the sacks that Henry had brought onto the ship. The lot left over by the pirates had nearly run dry, but she felt sure the rations that Henry had supplied would serve them well. While Henry steered the ship on deck, Elaine sorted through the sacks down below. But when she opened the first, Elaine's glistening green eyes widened in surprise. There was no more food on the ship, and the sacks that Henry had brought onboard were filled with treasure from the island.

Above deck, Henry looked out across the moonlit ocean, lifted his hand to see past the fog, and then spotted the Statue of Liberty in the distance. Overjoyed at the surmise of their long journey home, Henry raced down the staircase and burst through the door to tell Elaine. "We're home!" he shouted, rushing across the wooden floorboard until he reached her. "Elaine," he spoke, but she stood perfectly still, her eyes on the treasure. In her silent moments, when anything could have happened, Elaine terrified Henry the most.

"What's this?" Elaine prodded, sharply lifting

her head to meet his eyes.

"Elaine," Henry repeated, exhaling aloud. "We've reached New York. Did you not hear me?"

She held her tongue, ruminating, contemplating. When Henry understood her silence, it only took a moment longer for him to answer her original question.

"It's for us, Elaine," Henry declared. "I took it, so we could start our new life here. I want to take care of you, and I want you to be happy." Elaine pressed her lips together and sighed. "Can't you see what those coins can bring us? All of us?" Henry moved close enough to lay his hand over her stomach. "You must care what becomes of our child, Elaine."

"Yes," she relented. "I understand why you took it. I just wish you had told me."

Henry nodded, but his mouth remained closed.

"How much did you take? Is this all of it?"

"No. There was a great deal more, but I had no way of carrying it."

"I see," Elaine muttered, recalling the night Samson had accused her of moving the treasure. So much that had once been a muddled blur made sense all of a sudden, though it hardly mattered now.

"Elaine, there's nothing for you to fear anymore." Henry lifted her face in his hands and glanced down upon her with affection. "We're home now. And I promise, I'm going to take care of you - of us," he corrected, troubled by the thought of her unhappiness. But when she smiled, Henry relaxed at the sight. "Come," he encouraged, taking her hand. "Come with me."

\* \* \*

After abandoning the ship at the docks, Henry and Elaine trampled through the winter snow, searching for a place to stay the night. Despite their close proximity to the Rochester Mansion, Henry was ill-equipped to face his family just yet. For now, he needed a warm place to lie, where he could hold Elaine in his arms and convince her that her troubles would remain on the island, until he decided the next step to take.

Discovering an inn with numerous vacancies, Henry offered up a lump sum of gold, which was gladly received in exchange for a spacious room, fresh food, and silence. Henry and Elaine were covered in filth, reeking with the essence of the ship and sea. But the innkeeper had asked no questions, a pleasantry that Henry had generously rewarded with a handful of jewels.

Once Henry entered the room and locked the door behind them, he drew the curtains to block the moonlight from casting shadows across the furniture. Henry lit a few candles, while Elaine looked around in a state of disorientation, sitting down on the bed to keep from losing her balance. Of all the time spent away from civilized society, where people slept in houses and rode in carriages, Elaine had not expected to feel so comfortable with the life she had once lived. The streets of New York had not been beneath her feet since she was a little girl, and yet she felt as though only a day had passed since it had.

Henry ran a hot bath in the adjoining lavatory, then strolled back into the bedroom. In such a quick amount of time, he already felt at home in New York again, as if he had just left, as if he had never been gone at all. He could only hope that Elaine accepted the new, distantly familiar territory just as easily.

Unbuttoning his shirt, Henry held out a free hand to Elaine and said, "Join me."

She followed him into the lavatory, where he helped her out of her clothes after taking off his own. As she stepped into the warm water, her skin rejoiced at the luxurious feeling, because nearly a decade had passed since her body had been treated in such an elegant, sophisticated manner. Henry sat down in the tub behind her and proceeded to wash her back with soap and water, while she pulled her knees into her chest.

"You've been awfully quiet," Henry noted, delicately scrubbing the back of her neck.

Elaine looked out of the corner of her eye, though she hadn't even glimpsed Henry.

"Are you all right, Elaine?" Henry dipped his hand into the water, and then rinsed Elaine's neck and back. When she kept quiet, he placed his chin on her shoulder and wrapped his arm around her stomach. "You're safe with me, Elaine," he assured her. "Everything will be better now, I promise."

Elaine cleared her throat, then responded, "Why do you keep promising me things, Henry?"

Surprised by the question, Henry glanced down at Elaine's face and wondered how many worrisome thoughts were racing through her mind. "Because I want you to trust me, and I know you will."

Tears blurred Elaine's vision, as she casually blinked them away, hoping that Henry wouldn't notice. For so long, she had depended on herself alone, with Jade being the only exception to the rule. Now that Henry had provided her with so much - plans, hopes, promises - guilt had invaded her.

Was she worthy of Henry's love? Had she ever been? Elaine had made so many mistakes regarding Henry on the island, mistakes that she had rather take back but couldn't. Her mind was muddled and confused, as she had yet to grasp the possibility that they could start over and truly be happy here.

"I love you, Henry." Elaine turned her head over her shoulder to look back at him.

Henry stared into her eyes and opened his mouth to speak, but there were no words. Only wonder. Only enchantment. Only truth. Elaine was all he had ever wanted and all he would ever need, but he could never fathom the lucid depth of thought that was perpetually circling her brain. He could not understand her mind, because, in some ways, it was so unlike his own. Regardless, he wanted her forever and knew that there was enough love between them to mend whatever differences had arisen between them on the island.

"I should have told you more," Elaine realized. "I should have told you sooner. I'm sorry."

Grinning, Henry cupped Elaine's cheek in his hand and shook his head from side to side.

"Don't be sorry, my love. I knew what you felt for me, even before you did."

Henry lathered her arms with soap, and then poured water over her skin, as she finally began to relax. Closing her eyes, Elaine let Henry bathe her, cleanse her, take care of her, in a way that she needed to be cared for at the time, and in a way that Henry most definitely wanted to. Once they were both clean and stripped of any elements that had lingered from their time in the jungle and at sea, Henry dried Elaine off with a soft, plush towel and wrapped it around her body. Yawning, Henry cloaked himself with a towel of his own, then draped his arm around her shoulder, as they sauntered into the bedroom.

Feeling the bitter chill of winter in the air, Elaine let Henry take her towel, and then slipped beneath the warm covers of their great big bed. Henry hung the towels up to dry in the lavatory, before treading back into the bedroom and blowing out the candles. Elaine moved over, making room for Henry, as he lay down beside her in the bed and pulled her body into his embrace. Overwhelmed with exhaustion, Elaine put her head on Henry's chest and splayed her hand over his stomach, content to be nestled against his warm, bare skin.

For the first time, they fell asleep at precisely the same moment, too tired to let either of their minds wander with thoughts about the other. Instead, there was no more than the steady breathing of Henry and Elaine, peacefully sleeping in each other's arms. Neither had ever felt more secure.

## Chapter 29

When morning came, Henry and Elaine had yet to notice, still lost in the slumber that results after such a long voyage. By mid-afternoon, Henry stirred awake and thought about all that was left to do before visiting the Rochester Mansion. In those quiet moments of solitude, he watched Elaine as she slept, because nothing had ever brought him more peace.

Henry waltzed into the lavatory and took another bath while Elaine was resting, basking in the comforts of modern society. When he stepped out of the tub, Henry wrapped a towel around his waist and knotted the fabric at his hip. Then he stood in front of the mirror and looked at the strange, unfamiliar man staring back at him. With a straight razor and shaving soap, Henry rid his face of the thick beard that he had grown during his time on the island. But afterwards, when not even the slightest trace of stubble remained, he found himself disliking the clean-shaven appearance of his face, because it no longer looked like him either.

There was a knock at the door, which caused Elaine to open her eyes and groan. Henry stopped in the doorway of the lavatory and yelled out, "Yes?"

"I've brought lunch and those things you asked for, Mr. Rochester," the innkeeper announced, her shrill voice sending a jolt of panic through Elaine's system. She sat upright in the bed and held the covers up to her neck, because the only clothes she had were dirty, and in a pile on the floor with Henry's.

"Just leave it outside the door, please," Henry replied. "And thank you."

"Yes, sir. Let me know if you need anything else, Mr. Rochester."

The clink of a metal tray sounded, as the innkeeper set everything down outside the door. Henry pressed his ear to the wood and listened for the sound of her dissipating footsteps. When silence resumed, he opened the door to pick up the lunch tray, and then kicked the two boxes she had left inside the room.

"What are those?" Elaine asked after Henry shut the door.

Henry set the lunch tray down on the table by the window, then retrieved the boxes and tossed them onto the bed. He opened them one at a time, showing Elaine all that each held. "A dress for you, a suit for me."

Elaine stroked her fingers across the velvet, then picked the dress up in her arms. A smile came across her face, as she studied the burgundy-colored fabric of the long-sleeved floor length gown. It was something she would have chosen herself, had she been given the option. Glancing back, she found a pair of shoes at the bottom of the box, as well as a smaller box filled with jewelry: earrings, a diamond bracelet, and a pearl necklace. There were also other accessories as well, necessary tools for the styling and wearing of her hair.

"She must have forgotten one," Henry assumed, moving to open the door again. "No, I did." He stepped inside the room and closed the door behind him, another box in his hand. "Coats," he said.

Henry deposited the unopened box on the table, then reclaimed the lunch tray and carried it to Elaine. They ate chicken salad sandwiches in bed, then nibbled on a plate of crackers and cheese. Afterwards, they shared a cup of tea, needing the energy to finish the day that had yet to begin.

Once Elaine was done with the meal, she brought her hand to Henry's cheek and felt of his new, freshly shaven face. Henry placed his hand over hers and watched her admire the way he looked.

"I miss the whiskers," Henry chuckled. "I had grown quite fond of them."

Elaine laughed in response, eyeing him ardently. "So had I."

* * *

The minister stood before Henry and Elaine, dictating the exchange of vows that was spoken between husband and wife. Before long, the two were placing gold wedding bands on each other's fingers, and then sealing the formal declaration of love with a passionate kiss. It was not the way either had ever planned to enter the bonds of holy matrimony, but at present, it was the only way they wanted to.

* * *

Night had fallen, by the time Henry and Elaine arrived at the Rochester Mansion. The coachman pulled to a stop at the side of the road, while Elaine looked out the window with fear in her eyes. The large estate frightened her, not because of its wide sweeping windows and refined architecture, but because of the people who were inside of it.

Elaine had no blood relatives left of her own. The Rochesters would be the closest thing to family that she could find. But what if Henry's mother disapproved of her? They had married without his parents' blessing. What would they think of this strange island girl who hadn't known civilization in nearly a decade? And now that Elaine was carrying Henry's child, it made her all the more uncertain of how they would receive her.

"Ready, my love?" Henry took Elaine's hand

and searched her worried green eyes.

"Yes," she rasped, her focus solely on the gloriously tall brick mansion that stood before them.

Henry kissed Elaine on the cheek, and then opened the carriage door. Still in disbelief, Henry glanced up at his family home, as his breath formed into clouds of white vapor before his face.

"Henry?" Elaine sat in the open carriage, staring at the back of Henry's head until he turned around to face her. Nervous, she grabbed Henry's arm and begged, "Don't tell them about the baby. Not yet."

"But-"

"Please, Henry." Elaine lowered her gaze, watching Henry underneath her thick black lashes.

"As you wish," he succumbed, holding his hand out for her to take. Elaine placed her fingers into his open palm and lingered on the carriage steps. "What should I tell them?"

Elaine looped her arm around Henry's elbow, as he led her down the short walkway and up the front steps, until they reached the door. Just as anxious, she pressed her lips together, and then whispered, "The truth."

An elderly lady opened the door, dressed in an apron with a dishcloth in her hand. "Why, hello, Henry."

"Marge!" Henry called. He crossed the threshold, pulled her into his embrace, and then kissed her lightly on the cheek. "How splendid it is to see you!"

"What are you doing home so soon?" she inquired, her full cheeks pink with blush. "We weren't expecting you until sometime this spring."

"Who is it?" a short, snippy voice sounded from above.

Henry and Elaine looked up to find Mrs. Rochester at the top of the staircase, clinging to the banister. She descended the stairs like a sly, slinking creature, too calm to be trusted. Once she spotted Henry in the doorway, Mrs. Rochester froze in place, then glared down at her son.

"So, you've decided to come home, after all. The high seas weren't to your liking?"

"Come in out of the snow," Marge said, ignoring Henry's mother.

Elaine stood behind the threshold, feeling sick to her stomach. Noticing the look on Elaine's face, Henry grabbed her hand and pulled her into the foyer before Marge closed the front door.

"That will be all, Marge," Mrs. Rochester demanded. "You may return to the kitchen. Dinner won't fix itself." Marge curtsied before Henry and Elaine, but they did no more than smile. Once she left the room, Mrs. Rochester's beady eyes settled on Elaine, then drifted to her hand, which Henry was now holding.

"Hello, Mother," he kindly acknowledged, nodding in her direction.

"Why have you come home?" she bitterly remarked. "And where are the others? Or did you and Charles abandon them at sea?"

Henry scowled at his mother, as she narrowed her eyes at Elaine. Of all the ways she could have greeted his new bride, Henry had not expected this. When Elaine's nails dug into his hand, Henry wrapped his arm around her waist instead.

"They're all dead, Mother," Henry plainly spoke. "The captain, the crew, even Charles."

Mrs. Rochester held a hand over her gaping mouth, her eyes watering at the certainty of his words. After a moment, she closed her eyes and placed a hand to her chest. "What happened?" she breathed.

"There was a storm," Henry began, as Mrs. Rochester sat down on the staircase. "It destroyed the ship and killed everyone onboard. They all drowned, you see. And by some miracle, I survived."

"Oh, good God," Mrs. Rochester uttered, her fingers trembling as she raised them to dry her eyes.

"Yes," Henry sighed. "God is good, indeed. I washed ashore on an island and met Elaine," he explained, turning his head towards her. "She had been stranded there for years, because all of her family died in a shipwreck as well."

Elaine offered a faint smile, though felt sure that Henry's mother didn't approve of her. Mrs. Rochester appeared so cold and demeaning. How could she ever welcome a stranger with affection and love?

"Oh, Henry." Mrs. Rochester flickered her eyes over Elaine, then held her head in her hands.

"We've found our way home, Mother, and I couldn't be happier." Henry waited for a response, but there was none. "Where is Father? I should like to speak with him."

Mrs. Rochester raised her head, only for the purpose of staring at Elaine. "Why have you brought her here?" she wondered, her chin held high in pompous conceit.

"Because I'm his wife," Elaine answered, tired of being scrutinized by Henry's mother. Who was she to judge anyone, much less the woman who was carrying her grandchild? After surviving the jungle, killing two men, and watching Jade die in her arms, Elaine had nothing to fear. Mrs. Rochester no longer intimidated Elaine, because she was no longer capable of being intimidated.

Mrs. Rochester's eyes widened in astonishment, as she returned to Henry for confirmation.

"It's true," he said. "I love her, Mother, and you will accept her as part of this family."

"Mother," a light, curious voice called from the second floor. "Who's there?"

When Mrs. Rochester made no reply, a beautiful girl glided down the staircase, her voice brightening once she saw who stood in the foyer. "Henry!" she exclaimed, rushing forward to see her elder brother.

"Louisa!" Henry took his sister in his arms,

stroking his fingers through her long golden locks, as she sobbed into his chest. "Don't cry, darling."

"Oh, Henry," she stammered. "I didn't think you were ever coming back. Were you that unhappy here with me?"

"No, dear." Henry held Louisa at arm's length, then removed a handkerchief from his jacket for her to dry her eyes with. "It was no fault of yours. Now, stop crying. There is someone that I would like for you to meet." Henry rested his hand on Elaine's back and announced, "This is Elaine Carmichael. Excuse me, Elaine Rochester, my wife."

Louisa raised her hands to her mouth and screamed. "Oh, how wonderful!" Ecstatic, Louisa wrapped her arms around Elaine and pulled her into a warm embrace. "I've always longed for a sister."

Henry chuckled, as Elaine's chin landed on Louisa's shoulder. Louisa patted her sister-in-law's back and smiled up at Henry, much to Mrs. Rochester's dismay. At sixteen, she had enough cheer and fiery spirit to keep her mother's pessimistic opinions far away.

When Louisa pulled back, it was only so she could grab Elaine's hand with one of her own and Henry's with the other. "How did you meet? When did you return? Oh, please tell me everything."

"Another time, Louisa," Henry agreed. "But I promise to tell you everything."

Louisa clapped her hands together and bounced up and down. Her blue eyes had never been more lively and vivacious, because she had missed Henry so terribly while he was away. As much as Henry had loathed his mother's rush to find him a wife, Louisa was Mrs. Rochester's daughter, so the pressure to acquire a spouse was applied far more frequently.

"I'll get Father," Louisa volunteered. "Oh, Henry! Won't he be so delighted to see you? You as well, Elaine." Louisa grinned at the two of them, then took off running. Her voice could be heard throughout the house, as she called for Mr. Rochester down the hall.

"Well," Mrs. Rochester lilted, "you are pretty, I suppose." She rose from the staircase and found herself envying the fact that Elaine was taller than her. When Mrs. Rochester reached her hand out to touch Elaine's cheek, Henry grabbed his mother's wrist.

"If you so much as say one unkind word to her, I will see to it that it is the last unkind word to ever leave your lips." Henry's brown eyes glazed over his mother's face in a clear, powerful warning.

Mrs. Rochester took a step back, as Henry dropped her wrist. In that moment, Mr. Rochester entered the foyer with Louisa, and his wife conveniently took it upon herself to leave the room.

"Henry!" Mr. Rochester beamed at the sight of his only son, so thrilled to see him. "We weren't expecting you until March at the earliest." He embraced Henry, then swept away the traces of snow that remained on his son's shoulders. "I'm so glad you decided to shorten your trip and come home early."

When Henry saw his father take notice of Elaine, happiness flooded through him. At this point, Henry could care less about what his mother may think. His father's blessing, on the other hand, would mean the world to him.

"And who might this be?" Mr. Rochester wondered, straightening what was left of his silver hair. He was a tall, thin man, with long legs and arms. But his kindness was something that Elaine could sense without even looking at him.

"Father, I would like to introduce you to Elaine, or Mrs. Henry Rochester."

Mr. Rochester's eyes widened in surprise, though the smile remained.

"My wife," Henry clarified.

"I'm very pleased to meet you," Mr. Rochester said, while Louisa stood off to the side, looking on with wonder. "She's beautiful, Henry. I can see now why you chose to shorten your trip."

Henry exhaled, then met his father's eyes with absolute sincerity. "I didn't shorten my trip, Father."

"No? Then how come your arrival was so unexpected?"

"It's a long story," Henry admitted.

"Fine then," his father countered. "I'd be

pleased to hear it at dinner."

## Chapter 30

**H**enry, I don't know how you survived it," Mr. Rochester insisted. "Surely, no other has ever lived to tell such a tale." He adjusted a pair of wire-rimmed glasses over his nose, then returned to the food on his plate.

"Surely," Mrs. Rochester snorted.

Elaine set her napkin on the table, as all of the color drained from her face. Over the last hour, she had grown increasingly weak and needed to rest. The baby was taking more from her than she had anticipated.

"Are you all right, dear?" Mr. Rochester asked, his face wrinkling with concern.

"I'm feeling rather tired. I would like to lie down." Elaine tried to maintain her composure, but could feel it beginning to slip away. If only she could have a moment to herself in peaceful solitude and silence.

"Of course, darling." Henry stood up and pulled her chair back. She rose to take his hand

and felt very unsteady, but would not admit to her condition until her body tipped over to the side. "Elaine!" Henry gasped, reaching out to catch her in his arms as she fainted.

"Oh dear," Mrs. Rochester breathed. "Is she unwell?"

Henry brushed Elaine's hair out of her face and pressed the back of his hand to her forehead. "I don't know."

"Henry," Louisa inhaled, afraid for Elaine.

"I'm sure she's just exhausted, Henry," his father assured him. "Take her upstairs to rest, and she will be better by morning." Henry exchanged a worried glance with Louisa, who obviously shared his immediate concern for Elaine.

"Do as your father says, Henry." Mrs. Rochester took a gulp of wine from her glass. "Take her to one of the guest rooms upstairs. She'll be much more comfortable there."

"No," Henry protested, picking Elaine up in his arms. He clenched his jaw and glowered at his mother from across the table. "She is my wife," he growled, "and she will sleep in *my* room."

Henry carried Elaine out of the dining room and took her to his lofty bedroom upstairs. Kicking the door closed behind them, Henry laid her body down on the bed, and then slipped out of his jacket. Before he could think of what to do next, there was a knock on the door.

"Leave us alone!" Henry demanded, raising his voice.

"It's me, Henry," a small voice uttered from behind the door.

Henry took several long strides and opened the door. If he had known it was Louisa knocking, he wouldn't have barked at her so loudly. Of all the relatives in the Rochester Mansion, his sister was his favorite.

"I'm sorry, Louisa," he murmured. "You may come in." Henry stepped back to allow her entrance into his bedroom, and then shut the door once more.

"Father would like to speak with you in his study," Louisa informed him.

"What about?" Henry situated his hands on either side of his waist and turned back to Elaine, his mind distracted by fear and flooded with worry. What if she were ill from their time at sea? What if the weather had been too much for her? What if the baby-?

"He did not say," Louisa replied.

Henry turned back to Elaine and sighed.

"I'll sit with her," Louisa offered. "Father is anxious to see you."

Sitting down on the edge of the mattress, Henry touched the back of his knuckles to Elaine's cheek and observed her silent breathing. She looked like an angel when she slept, and for that, among other reasons, Henry had always done his best to treat her like one.

Louisa approached the bed and placed a hand on Henry's shoulder, but his eyes were on Elaine.

"You really love her," she observed. "Don't you?"

"Yes," Henry whispered. "I have never felt for any woman what I feel for her. She is everything to me, Louisa. My whole world. There has never been anyone for me but her."

"I'm glad," Louisa confessed. "Truly, I am."

"Thank you, Louisa." Henry clasped the hand on his shoulder and looked up at her. "You have always seemed much older than your age suggests. I believe you inherited that trait from Father."

"No." She smiled. "I learned it from you."

Henry mirrored her expression, then rose from the bed and placed his hands on his hips. "I hate leaving her," he confessed, "even for a moment. We're only apart when we have to be. What would you call that?"

"Oh, I don't know. Love, perhaps. But you already know that, Henry."

Amused, Henry glanced down at his young sister and grinned. In his time away, she had grown even wiser, more accomplished, more aware, more womanly. One day, she would be the kind of mother that Elaine would be, Mrs. Rochester should have been, and every hopeful girl could be.

"Go, Henry," Louisa insisted, interrupting his thoughts. "I'll watch over Elaine. I promise."

Henry was reluctant at first, but Louisa placed a reassuring hand on his arm, and he succumbed.

"Don't let her out of your sight," Henry commanded, pointing to Elaine's resting figure on the bed.

"I won't." Louisa smiled, then wrapped her arms around him. Taken aback, Henry held his sister close as she rested her head against his chest and sobbed quietly. "I'm happy for you both, but I'm even happier to see you home. I've really missed you, Henry."

"I've missed you, as well, but there is no need to cry, Louisa." Henry tugged her chin up and looked down at her, noticing the tears in her eyes. "I promise never to board another ship for the rest of my life."

"That is a promise you must keep."

* * *

After leaving Elaine in the care of his loving sister, Henry closed the bedroom door behind him and silently sauntered down the staircase. Glass encased candles were situated on either wall, as Henry made his way through the house, observing the wide, overwhelming hallways that he had never fully appreciated. Once Henry reached his father's study, he opened the cracked door and stepped inside.

"Henry," Mr. Rochester beckoned, motioning for him to sit down at the chair in front of his desk. When he did, Mr. Rochester removed his glasses and studied Henry very carefully. "So, you've found yourself a lovely young bride, I see." He leaned back in his chair and folded his hands over his stomach.

"Yes, Father." Henry offered an innocent grin, feeling disconnected from this old, yet new world of his.

"I am pleased by your return, Henry, and I approve of the marriage. Despite what your mother says, I do believe you and Elaine will make a fine life together."

"Thank you, Father." Henry beamed, delighted to have his blessing. "I believe so, as well."

Mr. Rochester rested his left forearm along the surface of his desk and pressed his right hand to his head. "I want to discuss something with you, Henry."

Henry furrowed his brow in anticipation, and then said, "Yes."

"You are a husband now, Henry. And as such, you will have a family to take care of and provide for sooner than you realize." Mr. Rochester opened one of the desk drawers and grabbed a packet of papers. "I am giving you your inheritance, as well as your stake in the family business."

"Father, I-"

"Listen, Henry," Mr. Rochester scolded. "I am an old man, and you have an obligation to this family."

"I would like to join the business immediately, Father," Henry revealed.

Mr. Rochester sat back in his chair and blinked. "Oh."

"But I cannot claim my inheritance while you are alive and well. Besides, we won't need it."

Offended, Mr. Rochester raised his eyebrows and turned his ear to the side, in case he had misheard his firstborn. "Excuse me, Henry. What did you say?"

Looking around the room, Henry dug into the pocket of his pants and held out his hand. Mr. Rochester's eyes widened in pure shock, as he stared down at the gold and jewels in Henry's palm. Once he had looked long enough, Henry returned the treasure to his pocket and resumed the conversation.

"You see, Father-"

"Henry, how on earth did you...?" Mr. Rochester lost his train of thought, wondering if he had imagined it.

"Never mind how I acquired them," Henry said. "Just rest assured, Father, that Elaine and I will be well taken care of. The business will remain safely in my hands when you are gone. Until then, there is no need for me to inherit anything, while you are still alive and well."

"Henry," Mr. Rochester sighed in disbelief.

"You must tell no one of what I have shown you. Do you understand me, Father?" Henry pointed a finger at the man he had spent his entire life looking up to. For the first time, Mr. Rochester was utterly speechless in the presence of his son. He couldn't comprehend what must have happened for Henry to acquire wealth in such a rare, unaccustomed form. What had Henry done while he was away?

"Yes." Mr. Rochester nodded. "I will tell no one."

"Even Mother," Henry pressed, eyeing his father carefully.

"Of course, Henry. Even your mother."

* * *

When Henry found Elaine awake upstairs, he couldn't have been happier. Louisa left them alone and scurried off to her own bedroom, content with the assurance that Henry had found love in the world. If only she could find such a romance for herself, so she could share the same joy.

"How are you feeling?" Henry shut the door behind him, then sat down beside Elaine in the bed. Resting had returned the color to her cheeks, though she appeared just as tired.

"Better," she muttered, softly smiling up at Henry. "Your sister, Louisa?"

"Yes?" Henry tilted his head to the side and widened the smile on his face.

"I like her," Elaine admitted, much to Henry's approval.

"You do?"

"Yes, she is one of the kindest people I have ever met."

Henry lay down beside Elaine and took her in his arms. Closing her eyes, Elaine placed her head on Henry's chest and relaxed at the feel of his fingers combing through her hair. She recalled that he had always been extremely gentle with her, during moments like these, and she loved that about him.

"Will you be happy here, my love?" Henry watched Elaine open her eyes, as she gazed up at him.

"Here?" She pulled her brows together, waiting for further clarification.

"In New York," he said, "with me."

"Yes, but you aren't planning to keep me in your mother's house. Are you?"

Henry stroked the stubble on his chin and chuckled. "No. We're getting a place of our own."

## Epilogue

Elaine welcomed spring with all of the warmth and kindness that it provided her with. The year was 1900, and Henry could hardly believe that either of them had lived to see the century change. Regardless, Henry and Elaine were equally filled with joy, because a new addition to the Rochester family would be arriving in June.

Brightened by the light of day, Elaine and Henry shared breakfast out on the veranda, where they could bask in the morning sunshine. After gathering his bearings, Henry had purchased a lovely estate in the country, flourishing with vast grounds and lush gardens. He felt sure that Elaine would be too confined by the limitations of city life, so the country had been the perfect place to take up residence.

"Are you feeling better?" Henry glanced across the table at Elaine, then lifted a cup of tea to his lips and drank. Her pregnancy had been a difficult one, but neither focused on that reality for very long.

"Yes, I believe I am." Elaine gazed out at the beautiful grounds before them, her thoughts drifting to the jungle, as they often did when she embraced the outdoors. Despite the lovely gardens and freshly cut grass, Elaine missed the wild, untamed thickets of the jungle. And she missed her life with Jade.

"Well, look who it is," Henry chimed, as a small black kitten walked out onto the veranda and approached Elaine. "I thought you wanted her for a house cat," he recollected.

Elaine bent down and picked the kitten up in her arms, while a tiny silver bell rang noisily on its collar. Once she placed the kitten in her lap, Elaine stroked the fur beneath its chin and behind its ears with her fingers. The kitten purred up at her, widening and narrowing a pair of liquid green eyes.

"I never asked for her, Henry," Elaine reminded him. "You brought her to me."

"As a gift," Henry said. He had seen the kitten through a store window and immediately thought of Elaine. Though a domestic breed, the kitten had the same black coat, green eyes, and untamed spirit as that wild jungle cat of hers had possessed. Henry knew that Elaine was still mourning the loss of Jade, so the kitten provided a chance to remember all that Elaine had left behind in the jungle.

"Have you thought of a name for her yet?"

Henry wondered, observing Elaine's lacy white fingerless gloves, as her hands traveled over the kitten's dark glossy fur.

"No." Elaine smiled down at the kitten, as she kneaded her paws in delight.

"Well." Henry sat up in his chair. "We could call her Ja-"

"NO!" Elaine's lively green eyes turned to Henry, trapping him with an enraged look of fury.

"I was just-"

"We're not naming her that," Elaine demanded, as her focus returned to the kitten in her lap. "In fact, I'd rather not name her at all. And I'm not entirely fond of this collar around her neck either." She unclasped the collar and dropped it onto the table beside a tray of biscuits and strawberry preserves. "There," Elaine sighed, holding the kitten to her chest, "that's much better."

Henry bit his tongue, quietly returning to the eggs and sausage that remained on his plate. He cut into the meat with his knife and fork, then ate every last scrap of food on the table. When Elaine had yet to break the silence, Henry wiped his mouth with a cloth napkin and tossed it over his empty plate.

Elaine set the kitten down on the veranda and watched as she scampered through the garden, before disappearing into the wilderness. The collar remained on the table, as well as the silver bell that could have informed others of the kitten's whereabouts, in case she should get lost on the property.

"We'll never find her," Henry supposed, frustrated and disgruntled.

"She'll come back." Elaine toyed with the bell on the collar and giggled. "Besides, I want her to be free," she said, looking off to the wilderness. "If I were a cat, I would want to be free."

"I fear that I will never understand your mind, my darling," Henry muttered, chewing on his meal.

Holding her chin high, Elaine looked across the table at Henry and crossed her arms over her chest. "Imagine if someone put a chain around your neck," she reasoned. "How would you feel?"

"A package has arrived, Mr. Rochester," the butler announced, appearing before them on the veranda.

"Leave it in my room, please. That will be all." Henry dismissed the butler, then returned his focus to Elaine. "Expecting anything?" he asked her, his curiosity increasing by the second.

"No," she answered. "Nothing."

After breakfast, Henry and Elaine stood in front of a wooden table, where the package was waiting for them. Disinterested, Elaine sprawled out on the large bed they shared and let her head sink into the soft pillow. When Henry showed no intention of joining her, she watched him from where she lay.

"Well, open it," Elaine declared. "It's only a

box."

Henry paced the floor, finding it odd that the package possessed no return address, and that the handwriting was unrecognizable. Since he could do no more than stand there, Elaine climbed off the bed and marched towards him, her fluctuating hormones proving worthy. "What do you think?" Henry asked.

Elaine scoffed at him and eyed the box like it was the object of a predator, but more importantly, her prey. "If you refuse to open it, then I will. Perhaps another relative sent a belated wedding gift."

"That's highly unlikely," Henry mused.

Determined to discover what lay inside, Elaine tore the lid off the box, and then set it down on the table. Her heart jolted forward, nearly knocking her off balance, when she saw that the package had been filled entirely with sand. Henry touched Elaine's arm as they both froze in place, sharing a cursory glance before their eyes returned to the inside of the box.

"Henry," Elaine rasped, her throat so dry that she could hardly breathe.

Curious, Henry removed his jacket, and then rolled his shirtsleeves up until they reached his elbows. Before Elaine could question him, Henry stuck his hands deep into the sand and felt of something hard at the center. Perplexed, he clasped the object in his hands, pulled it out of the sand, and set it down on the table.

As soon as every trace of sand had cleared away, Elaine let out a piercing shriek, quickly succumbing to a fit of hysteria. Henry grasped her shoulders and attempted to pull her body into his embrace, but she flung her arms about, crying and moaning. The butler and maid both rushed into the room, terrified by the sound of Elaine's screeching voice. They turned to look at Henry, who was still trying to console her. When he finally did, she buried her face into his chest and let him hold her.

Henry glanced back at the staff, then darted his eyes towards the object that sat on the table. "Get rid of it."

All eyes, apart from Elaine's, remained on that mysterious item for some time. Because, at the center of the room, atop the table, was a plain glass jar filled with salt water, ocean water, water from the sea. And floating in that water, like some ghost of a nightmare, were a pair of familiar eyes.

*Beautiful* eyes. *Green* eyes. *Jungle* eyes.

They were the eyes of a beloved black panther, who had once been called Jade.

## Tell Me Your Favorite Part!

If you enjoyed Jungle Eyes, I invite you to head over to Amazon and let me know your favorite part. Reviews are so important to an author's career, because they help new readers like you discover the book. Even if you didn't enjoy Jungle Eyes, I'd still love it if you could take three minutes to let me know what you think of the book.

## Leaving a review is super easy:

1) Go to Jungle Eyes Book Page on Amazon

2) Scroll Down and click "Write a Customer Review"

3) Sign in to Amazon if prompted

4) Select a star rating

5) Write a few short words (or long words, I won't judge)

6) Click the 'submit' button

I thank you in advance!

## Acknowledgements

Much thanks to the supportive network of family and friends, who have encouraged me, challenged me, and never stopped believing in me. Your kind, reassuring words have been so futile in helping me chase after my dreams. I cannot thank each of you enough.

To Larissa at *The Howling Turtle*, Naylene at *More than Scribbles*, Aly at *Reading Shy with Aly*, Matthew at *Bibliofreak*, Em at *Afternoon Bookery*, Dani at *Paulette's Papers*, Ailyn at *Penny for My Thoughts*, Amanda at *Girl with a Pen and a Dream*, Yvonne at *Socrate's Book Reviews*, Claire Hill, L. T. Kelly and S. K. Gregory. Thank you for the features, spotlights, interviews, guest posts, and reviews. I am highly indebted to you all.

Also, I would like to send a tremendous amount of warmth and gratitude to the reader. Without you, these novels would just be a collection of daydreams in my mind. Whether you are a fan of Tom and Addie, Cabel and Finley, or Henry and Elaine, I am pleased to say that all of their stories have plenty of new chapters to come. Stay tuned.

## About the Author

Lindsay Marie Miller was born and raised in Tallahassee, Florida, where she graduated from high school as Valedictorian. At sixteen, she started writing her first novel, *Emerald Green*, after being inspired by Stephenie Meyer's International Bestselling *Twilight Saga*. During her time in college, Lindsay wrote 5 more novels and over 100 songs. After graduating Summa Cum Laude from Florida State University, she put her B.A. in English Literature to good use and published her debut novel, *Emerald Green*. An author of over 10 Romance Titles, Lindsay currently resides in her hometown of Tallahassee where she is always working on her next novel.

### To learn more, please visit:

www.lindsaymariemillerauthor.com

### Sign up for Lindsay's newsletter:

lindsaymariemillerauthor.com/claim-your-free-book/

### Join Lindsay on Facebook at:

facebook.com/LindsayMarieMillerAuthor

### Follow Lindsay on Twitter at:

twitter.com/Lindsay_MMiller

Here's a sneak peek of

# ISLAND SMILE,

the heart pounding sequel.

# Chapter 1

It was a warm summer night in the country when Elaine Rochester curled her knees into her swelling stomach and gasped. A hand went over the large bump, her fingers pressing into the soft fabric of her night gown. But then the cramping, tightening sensation worsened as she rose into an upright position by her husband on the bed.

Awakened by the noise, Henry sat up and whispered, "Elaine?"

Wincing from the discomfort, Elaine turned onto her side and pressed the edge of her face into the mattress. Heat flushed across every surface of her skin in strong flames.

"Elaine, what is it my darling?" He touched her shoulder delicately. "What's wrong?"

"The baby," she replied with a shallow breath. "The baby is coming."

"I'll call for the doctor." Henry ripped the sheet back and leapt down from the bed.

Elaine yelped in pain with the arrival of

another contraction, stopping Henry in his tracks. "Go, Henry!" she demanded. "What are you waiting for? Call the doctor!"

Not wanting to abandon her, Henry stood there contemplating the consequences of leaving her alone and then scurried into the hallway. After making a frantic phone call to the doctor, Henry bolted downstairs and woke Martha, their most trusted house servant. She lifted the skirt of her night gown as Henry rushed her up the staircase, rattling off every immediate thought that came crashing into his mind.

When the doctor arrived, Henry kept at his heels, aimlessly tugging at his elbow. "Do you think she is in a great deal of pain?" Henry prodded and probed.

"Henry," the doctor sternly declared, turning back to him at the entrance of their bedroom. "She is about to give birth. Of course she is in pain." The doctor patted Henry's shoulder and then continued into the room with Martha.

"Yes, but—" Before Henry could finish, the door slammed in his face.

Taking a step back, Henry set his hands on his hips and exhaled. His light brown eyes raced across the floor as he turned around and began pacing it. Frantic and frustrated, Henry rubbed his palms together until they were slick with moisture, his heart pounding with every shrill cry of Elaine's voice. How ridiculous that he was not allowed to witness the birth of his own child. He was the father for goodness sake. It was absurd.

As the clock ticked on the wall, Henry took a seat in the long corridor, his brow brimming over with sweat. He lifted a shaky hand to swipe the smooth dark strands of fallen hair out of his face. But then Elaine screamed and Henry's head shot up at the agonizing sound. It was painful to listen to, and he imagined it must have been all the more painful to watch. Regardless, he wanted to be present and ease her current disposition in some fashion or form, even if her pain was the kind that could not be shared.

Henry took to pacing the floor again when Elaine cried out his name. His long fingers ran through his mane then over and across the stubble of his beard. Turning his head from side to side, Henry marched up and down the hallway until it sounded like he was stomping.

"Henry," Elaine crooned through the door. "I want Henry."

Desperate to draw near, Henry twisted the metal knob on the door and could hardly believe that it was unlocked. When he burst into the bedroom, Martha rushed forward with a stout palm in the air, blocking his entrance. "Mr. Rochester," she announced. "You aren't supposed to be in here."

"Henry," Elaine rasped. "Where is Henry?"

"I am here, my love." He turned to approach, but Martha stepped in the way.

"You are not allowed in here, Mr. Rochester,"

Martha reiterated. "Your presence is highly unacceptable."

"Henry," Elaine called again, her breathy voice shaky and distant.

"Let him in," the doctor ordered, impatient with the added distraction.

Though she did not agree, Martha stepped aside and allowed Henry to walk into the room. Once he brushed past her, Martha shut the door and all attention returned to Elaine.

"Henry," Elaine cried out, reaching her hand towards him.

"Yes, darling." Henry raced to her side, thankful that the doctor had overlooked his presence and willfully accepted it. "I'm here now." He knelt down on the floor beside Elaine and took her hand. "I'm here. I promise not to leave."

Elaine let out a breath of air as Henry gently kissed her forehead, glistening with beads of sweat. With another burst of pain, Elaine gasped and gritted her teeth. Henry thought the bones in his hand might break, but he dare not tell Elaine that she was squeezing too hard, that her grip had grown stronger, that she was hurting him. How could he complain when she was the one writhing in pain? If he must suffer too, then so be it.

For the next three hours, Elaine remained in a tortuous state of labor. Henry never left her side, but wondered if he had been selfish in causing her to carry and birth his child. Had he known the degree of pain she would be in, Henry might have considered the probability of procreation more somberly.

But her anguish and suffering were nature's price for the joyous infant she would soon bear. For months now, Elaine had shared her dreams with Henry. Dreams where they strolled through Central Park with a newborn child. A little girl. Sometimes two.

These dreams had visited Elaine nearly every night since their return to New York. Henry hoped they were a sign of all the good things to come, the exciting new life they would live together, the fulfillment of a promise he had made her long ago on the island. But now, watching Elaine give birth to their child, Henry knew that a dream could be defined by more than those images that delight or haunt one's sleep.

Life was a dream.

Elaine was a dream.

And the precious life Henry had created with her was one as well.

That hot summer night, at the first sound of his daughter's piercing scream, Henry truly believed that all he had ever hoped for or wanted were his two beautiful girls.

Taken aback, Henry rubbed his chin and gazed at the sight of Elaine holding their precious newborn daughter in her arms. Elaine glanced down at the sleeping child with tears in her eyes, delicately touching her thumb to the baby's cheek. When she looked up at Henry, Elaine was pleased to find tears in his eyes as well.

"Would you like to hold her?" Elaine rubbed her lips together and smiled.

"Yes." Henry stepped forward, and Elaine gently placed the infant in the strength of his arms. As his eyes rushed over their bundle of joy, Elaine left her hand on Henry's arm. "What shall we call her?" he wondered, glancing back at Elaine.

Beaming with happiness, Elaine dried her eyes. "I thought of a name."

Henry cradled his daughter close to his chest, admiring her with fascination.

"You may not like it, Henry," Elaine feared, sitting upright in the bed.

"Won't you at least give me the chance to hear it?" he countered.

Elaine batted her long black lashes with a cat-like grin. "Lillian."

"Lillian," he echoed, letting the sound roll off his tongue.

"After my mother," Elaine continued. "Everyone always called her Lilly."

Henry watched their daughter as he replied, "Lilly it is then."

A silent tear slid down Elaine's cheek. She quickly wiped the moisture away and looked up at her husband holding her daughter in his arms. All those years she had spent stranded on the island alone with no one but Jade for comfort in the jungle, Elaine never could have imagined a life for herself. One where she had love and a home and a family.

Henry ambled towards the window, whispering sweet promises to Lilly all the while. As he placed the newborn child in her bassinet, moonlight shone through the nearest window. Henry closed the curtains to block out the evening glow, ready for the break of day even though it was the middle of the night. After planting a sweet kiss on his daughter's head, Henry returned to bed and slipped beneath the covers beside Elaine.

"How are you feeling, my love?" Henry lay down and combed his fingers through her black hair, hoping that whatever discomfort the pregnancy had caused would flee.

Without a word, Elaine stroked the edge of his jawline and smiled.

"What?" Henry cupped her cheek in his hand. "What is it?"

"I feel..." Her green eyes glistened with water in the night. "Happy."

With a crooked smile, Henry leaned closer and gifted a kiss on her lips.

"But something is wrong," Elaine said. "Something is not right, Henry."

"Darling," Henry whispered. "What on earth are you talking about?"

"The dreams. I have had dreams," she struggled with the words. "Dreams that I did not tell you about before. Dreams about you. Dreams about me. Dreams about the baby."

Henry dragged his knuckles across her cheek.

"What sort of dreams?"

"Something is coming. Someone is coming. It is not good, Henry."

Henry took her face in his hands, unsure of what comfort he could provide. How could he convince her that they were finally safe? That they would never have to survive in the jungle again? That all that had happened there was over? That it had been over?

"They are dreams, Elaine," he insisted. "Dreams and nothing more."

"But what if they aren't dreams?" She touched his hand and looked deep into his eyes. "What if it is real? What if they are all real?"

Henry swallowed. "Elaine, you've just had a child. You need rest."

"I can see it in your eyes," she murmured. "You think I'm mad. Don't you?"

Startled by his wife's premonition, Henry gazed across the room at Lilly asleep in her bassinette. He had hoped that the pregnancy had been the sole source of Elaine's dreams. Since leaving the island, Henry had noticed moments when Elaine was not quite herself.

There was sadness, emptiness, loss. All present in her glowing green eyes.

Was it Jade? The jungle? The ocean? The life they once had together?

And then there was the matter of that package. The sand. The jar. The water and what had been floating inside. Like two pieces of evidence cut from the beast with a knife.

"Elaine." Henry swept his thumb across the length of her cheek. "I told you that I will take care of you. I will shelter you. I will protect you."

Elaine lowered her lashes in response. "Promise me something, Henry."

"Yes." Henry shook his head ever so slightly. "Of course."

Elaine met Henry's lively gaze, then flicked her eyes to the bassinette before settling on Henry again. "Promise me that if you have to choose between us, you will choose her."

Henry turned his face and took in the sight of their helpless child, only an hour old.

"Promise me, Henry." Elaine squeezed his hand and dug her nails into his palm.

"No, Elaine." Henry's brows came together in frustration. "I will make no such promise." He pulled his hand from her grasp and placed it on her shoulder.

Elaine fought through her tears and mumbled, "But you must."

"No. No!" Henry sat back and narrowed his eyes. "I will never give you up."

When her lower lip trembled, Elaine tossed her head back and cried. Never intending to upset her, Henry smoothed his hands along the side of her arms and brushed his mouth against hers. Then he trailed a line of gentle kisses from cheek to cheek.

Elaine curled her hands around the back of

Henry's neck and clung to his warm body. As their torsos became flush, Henry cherished the tender embrace and rubbed her back. Her breath in his ear was a warm caress, reminding him of all that he had to lose.

"I love you, Henry," Elaine wept, resting her head in the crook of his neck.

Henry consoled her in the night, hoping more than believing that her emotions were no more than a natural reaction to giving birth. But as he held her body close, Henry sensed the fear flowing through her veins, because it was as palpable as a cool breeze in the wind.

Lying down with her head on his chest, Henry rubbed her arm and looked at the ceiling. Deep down, if he was completely honest with himself, Henry had felt it, too. Many months ago, when he had been foolish enough to let Elaine open that package.

"Listen to me, my love." Henry tilted his chin to glance down at her. "No one will ever take Lilly away from us." He watched her eyes, the way they glistened and gleamed.

Elaine placed her hand on his chest and counted on every word he said.

"And no one will ever take you away from me. Do you understand?"

Elaine offered a faint nod. "Yes, Henry. I understand."

"We are going to build a happy life here, Elaine. Just as I promised you." Henry tucked a jet black lock behind her ear and tugged her chin up with his thumb. "We are meant to be together. It is the only thing that makes sense. And it is the only thing that matters."

Nodding once more, Elaine kept her head on his firm chest and snuggled closer. Henry wrapped his arms around her back and listened to the sound of her breathing until she succumbed to her own weariness and drifted off. As he stroked his fingers through her hair, Henry decided that no one would lay a hand on his daughter or his wife.

Unless they wanted to gaze into the open end of his pistol.

## Chapter 2

One week passed and then two. With Elaine settling into the joys and obligations of a first time mother, Henry accepted an invitation for dinner at the Rochester Mansion. Since marrying and moving out to the country, Henry rarely found time for his mother and younger sister, Louisa. But he was thankful for the days with his father that the family business allowed. It was an ever-growing industry steepled in trade and commerce. One that Henry felt exceptionally proud and pleased to be a part of.

Upon arriving at the Rochester Mansion, Henry gazed out the carriage window and glanced up at the brick structure he had once called home. During his time on the island, Henry had accepted the fact that he might never see the place again. Now that they were back, he couldn't be sure what he had missed. The home he had made with Elaine in the country was the only place he hoped to spend the rest of his life.

Henry helped Elaine out of the carriage and led her to the front door, while she cradled Lilly in her arms, the sweet baby drifting off in a bundle of warm blankets. When Marge opened the door, Henry guided Elaine into the mansion and smiled. Not only was Marge the oldest member of the staff, she had lasted the longest, which meant she had more grit than the rest. Finding a servant to partake of Mrs. Rochester's unruly behavior was a task that not many could handle.

"Henry!" Louisa barreled down the staircase and leapt into her brother's arms, so filled with budding excitement at the ripe age of sixteen. Her blonde hair swayed as she ran, those long blonde curls tied back in a blue ribbon. She was especially ecstatic.

"Why my dear, sister." Henry set her down and held her at arm's length. "You sure are pleased to see us." He pinched her cheek and watched her bright eyes dart to Elaine.

"Hello Louisa," Elaine greeted, a healthy blush to her complexion.

Louisa stood silently in place, stopping and staring at the newborn child.

"Would you like to meet your niece?" Elaine could not help but grin, absorbing every bit of emotion flooding through Louisa's veins. It was a beautiful sort of fascination.

Louisa moved closer but remained hesitant, careful not to wake the baby. When she grew brave enough, Louisa reached out and touched the sleeve of Lilly's arm. A pleasant smile spread across her face, because Lilly had charmed her from the very start.

"She's so little," Louisa noted, inextricably captivated.

"She cries quite often as well," Henry added with a subtle whisper.

Louisa left her hand on Lilly's shoulder, unable to look away.

"Would you like to hold her?" Elaine wondered.

Louisa's blue eyes widened at the possibility. "May I?"

"Of course." Elaine cradled her daughter close as she gently placed her in Louisa's arms. With Lilly's head resting against her heart, Louisa could hardly contain the sense of pure love that had enveloped her. Deep down, she longed to become a mother one day and admired Elaine all the more for accomplishing the feat already.

Henry and Elaine shared an intimate look, acknowledging the way Louisa was so easily taken with their daughter. She was precious, the glue eternally binding Henry and Elaine to one another. Marriage was one thing. Love was another. But even with the two combined, nothing measured up to the delight of sharing a child.

"Oh, is that the baby?" Mrs. Rochester bustled into the room, worried that she had missed something. When she spotted her only grandchild pleasantly nestled in the arms of her only daughter, Mrs. Rochester held a hand to her mouth. A tear slid down her cheek as she welcomed the next branch on her family tree with limitless warmth.

"Henry, she's beautiful," Mrs. Rochester declared.

"Thank you, Mother." Henry gave her a kiss and hug, before she turned to Elaine and did the same. With the birth of Lilly, Mrs. Rochester's treatment of Elaine had turned from disgruntled to exemplary. Apparently, the addition of a grandchild worked wonders.

"She is beautiful, Elaine," Mrs. Rochester crooned, brimming over with newfound joy.

Elaine thanked her with a wide smile and then leaned into Henry's arm.

"Where is Father?" Henry put his hand along Elaine's waist, happy that the arrival of his firstborn was so well received. But he longed to witness his father's reaction.

"Hello, Henry." Mr. Rochester waltzed into the foyer and patted his son on the back. "Elaine," he acknowledged, offering a nod and hug. "What do we have here?"

Henry draped his arm across Elaine's shoulders as she settled into his embrace. "Your grandchild," he answered. "Lillian Carmichael Rochester."

"Look at her, Father," Louisa chimed. "Isn't she just beautiful?"

"Yes," Mr. Rochester admitted with a smile.

"Yes, she is."

As Lilly became acquainted with her grandparents, Elaine furrowed her brow in discomfort. Her eyes shot to the floor, though she was not staring at the surface beneath her feet. The dark thoughts were back, and they had returned stronger than ever before.

"Darling?" Henry smoothed his thumb along her cheek, perplexed by the look on her face. In the past week, her anxiety had lessened, but Henry recognized the slight line forming between her brows. She was afraid. Of what, he did not know.

Blinking rapidly, Elaine woke up from her daydream and looked into Henry's eyes. He threaded his long fingers through her black locks, offering what comfort he could.

"Are you all right, my love?" Henry cocked his head to the side.

"Yes." She moistened her lips and brushed the matter off. "I'm fine."

"Well." Mr. Rochester lingered in the foyer. "Shall we eat?"

"Yes!" Mrs. Rochester followed his lead as the two proceeded towards the dining room arm in arm. If not for Lilly in her arms, Louisa would have scurried after them.

"Would you like me to take the baby upstairs to rest?" Louisa asked.

"Yes, Louisa," Elaine muttered. "That will be fine."

Once she was up the staircase and out of sight,

Elaine turned back to Henry and clamped her hand around his arm. The blacks of her eyes were rapidly dilating.

"What is it?" Henry hissed, looking over his shoulder towards the dining room.

"Something is wrong, Henry." Elaine kept her voice low, assuming that anyone else in the mansion would mark her as mad if they overheard. "Something is not right."

"Elaine, whatever you are imagining, I can assure you that it is all in your head."

"No, Henry. Listen to me. Something is coming. Someone is coming."

"Henry!" Mrs. Rochester yelled from the dining room.

"Coming, Mother!" he called, turning back to Elaine. "Listen, darling." Henry cupped Elaine's cheeks in his large, strong hands. "You never spoke like this until the baby came. Perhaps that is what all of this is about."

Elaine tightened her grip on his arm. "You're not listening to me."

"The potatoes are getting cold!" Mrs. Rochester nagged with impatience.

"We'll be right there, Mother!" Henry yelled back down the hall.

When his attention returned to Elaine, the look on her face could have killed. "You don't believe me. Do you?" she inquired. "You think I'm simply imagining things."

"Elaine, I never said that," he defended,

clenching his jaw.

"You didn't have to." Elaine let go of his arm and climbed the staircase.

Henry watched her figure until she disappeared at the top of the steps. Frustrated and concerned, Henry stood there wondering how she could worry over something that was non-existent. Not only was the fear strange, it didn't even make sense.

"HENRY!"

"I'm coming!" Henry stormed down the hall and into the dining room, ready to devour whatever food he could get his hands on. As he took a seat, his eyes remained on the ceiling. He couldn't help but wonder what his wife and sister were discussing upstairs.

* * *

"Why Lilly?" Louisa wondered. "Where did the name come from?"

"It was my mother's," Elaine replied. "Lillian Carmichael. But she always went by Lilly. At least from what I can remember. I think of her often."

"Well, I think Lilly is a beautiful name." Louisa held out her pinkie for the baby to squeeze. Though her eyelids fluttered back and forth, Lilly was nearly awake, fighting sleep. When she opened her mouth and noticed Elaine, a bout of crying ensued.

"Oh, there now." Elaine swept the baby up in her arms and rubbed her back. "Is my sweet baby girl all right?" Holding her protectively close, Elaine lightly bounced the child until she fell back asleep. At the sight of peace on her face, Elaine placed Lilly in the crib Henry's father had specifically purchased for any time they might come by for a visit.

"Elaine, may I ask you something?" Louisa whispered, suddenly shy.

Undoubtedly curious, Elaine took a seat beside the crib and replied, "Of course." Then she took Louisa's hand in hers and gave it a reassuring pat. "We are sisters now."

"Yes," Louisa realized. "I suppose we are."

"Well..." Elaine motioned her hand in a circle. "Go on. Out with it."

"Someone else will be joining us for dinner tonight," Louisa revealed.

"Oh?" Elaine watched over Lilly for a moment. "Who?"

"Well." Louisa braided her fingers together and bit her lip. "I am in love."

"Love?" Elaine narrowed her eyes questioningly. "With whom?"

"A man named William." Louisa swooned and sighed, "William Pierce."

"William Pierce," Elaine repeated. "Who is that?"

"He is captain of a merchant ship," she boasted. "We met by accident a couple months ago. His carriage nearly crashed into mine, but mother blames our driver. We've kept the romance secret until now, and I didn't want to overwhelm you with it all."

"Do your mother and father know?"

"Why, yes! Of course," Louisa urged. "They were the first to know. And since William has already spoken with Father and received his permission—"

"What?" Elaine cut in, unsure how she felt about the news.

"Oh, Elaine. We are engaged!" Louisa jumped in place for a moment, hopping about the room like a frolicking bunny rabbit. "I have just been dying to tell you!"

"Engaged?" Elaine echoed, her pulse quickening with the word.

"Yes!" Louisa spun about the room. "Oh, isn't it wonderful?"

"Louisa, calm down," Elaine ordered. "Take a seat and listen to me."

Disappointed yet obedient, Louisa plopped down in the chair across from Elaine.

"How well can you possibly know this man?" she inquired. "What makes you so sure that this William Pierce is someone you can trust?"

"We've spent loads of time together. Just William and I. You will love him, Elaine."

Feeling queasy, Elaine grabbed Louisa's hand and said, "I just want to make sure that you are making the right decision for you. You are sixteen, Louisa. What is the rush?"

Louisa sat back in her chair and crossed her

arms over her chest. Her eyes were downcast, skirting across the floor, because she was wholly discouraged by Elaine's response. Looking up to her as a sister, Louisa had truly hoped for her approval.

"When I see the way Henry looks at you, I know that I want that for myself." Louisa lurched forward and wrapped her fingers around Elaine's arm. "I know everything is coming together rather quickly, but what does that matter when it is your true love?"

Elaine opened her mouth to speak, but Louisa kept on.

"He loves me, Elaine. He told me so himself. And I love him."

"Yes, but—"

"Oh, please," Louisa begged. "Please won't you be happy for me? For us?"

The doorbell rang as Elaine swallowed, her innermost feelings swelling with doom.

"Oh, he is here! How wonderful! Just as he said he would," Louisa cheered.

Before Elaine could speak another word, Louisa grabbed ahold of her wrist and dragged her into the hall and down the staircase. Mr. Rochester welcomed the evening guest with a friendly handshake, while Mrs. Rochester fawned all over him in the foyer.

"William!" Louisa sailed down the remaining steps and into his arms.

His back was turned to the banister, so Elaine

could hardly make out the sight of him, as the rest was blocked by Mr. and Mrs. Rochester. When Henry appeared from the dining room, Elaine joined him at the bottom of the staircase. "Who is this man?"

Elaine lowered her voice and replied, "I don't know."

"How I have missed you, my love," William cooed, gifting a sweet kiss on Elaine's forehead. He touched her cheeks with his hands as Henry gritted his teeth.

"Oh Henry, Elaine," Mr. Rochester called, his head popping up. "Come and meet William. He and your sister are engaged."

Henry and Elaine looked at one another before drawing near. As Mrs. Rochester stepped aside and looped her arm through her husband's, the esteemed merchant boat captain turned around for all in the room to see. His long blonde locks fell to his shoulders like a lion's mane, the rough, dark nature of his skin alluding to as much brutality.

"Hello there." He held out his hand politely. "My name is William Pierce."

Henry widened his eyes, while Elaine remained frozen in place like a block of ice. Neither could be sure if it were miracle or magic. Either way, the impossible was true.

Judas had returned from the dead.

## Chapter 3

**H**enry," Mrs. Rochester prompted. "Aren't you going to say something?"

Henry balled one hand into a fist at his side, a slick sheen of sweat breaking out across his forehead. Judas gently lifted the corners of his mouth into a teasing smirk, his cobalt irises flaring like cataclysmic waves in an endless sea. "That is quite all right, Mrs. Rochester. Perhaps the young lad is shy when meeting new strangers."

"No, William," Louisa countered. "Henry, you are being rude."

Tackling the situation head on, Elaine extended a hand and stepped between Judas and Henry. "Hello, sir. I am delighted to make your acquaintance."

Judas pinned Elaine to the spot with an unsettling stare, delicately taking her palm in his. "Charmed, I am sure." He brought his mouth to the back of her hand and then gave her fingers a light squeeze. "What a lovely young wife you have," he waited a beat, then added, "Henry."

Flames rippled across the surface of Henry's skin. In that moment, he had never wanted to pounce on another human being and rip the man's jugular out with his bare hands so much. With the force and claws of that jungle cat Elaine had always kept by her side.

"Hello, Mr. Pierce is it?" Henry shook Judas's hand with a painful grip.

"Yes." Judas gasped and withdrew his hand from Henry's constricting hold. "Captain William Pierce, actually. I am in charge of the merchant ship, La Fleur Noire."

"Is that French I detect?" Mr. Rochester guessed.

"Yes," Judas nodded. "I speak it fluently. French, German, Italian."

"What does it mean, my love?" Louisa hung on his every word like a helpless fool.

"La Fleur Noire?" Judas checked and she nodded. "The black flower."

"How lovely and poetic," Louisa murmured, batting her eyes up at him.

"Well, dinner has been served. Let's continue this conversation in the dining room." Mr. Rochester steered his wife in that direction as Louisa and Judas followed suit. On the walk down the hall, the latter turned back and winked at Henry over his shoulder.

Once they were gone, Henry spun around to face Elaine. "Tell me I have gone mad. Or did you just see what I seem to have seen?" He held her gaze perceptively.

Elaine flicked her eyes to the empty hall and then grabbed Henry by the wrist, dragging him into the drawing room. With her heart pounding, Elaine shut the French doors and looked back to find Henry pacing the floor. Neither could understand why, at the exact moment William's true identity had been discovered, they had failed to utter a single word.

"How can that man be standing on his own two feet? Alive?" Henry pointed a long finger towards the front of the house, as furious as he was disturbed.

"I killed him." Elaine's worried green eyes dropped to the floor. "I thought I killed him."

"You did," Henry emphasized. "I saw his dead body with my own eyes."

"But I stabbed him in the chest," Elaine recalled. "More than once. I stabbed him in the heart. How could any man overcome something like that? He must be dead."

"What if it isn't him? What if we have both gone mad? Lost our minds?"

"No, Henry." Elaine placed her hands on his shoulders and gazed into his eyes. "It was real. All of it. Everything that happened on the island. I just can't comprehend how—"

"Maybe it's not him," Henry suggested. "Perhaps a brother, a twin?"

"A twin with the same scar on his cheek?"

"I didn't notice it," Henry confessed, narrowing his eyes in confusion.

"Perhaps you should look closer next time."

Henry exhaled aloud and moved away from Elaine, running his fingers through his hair. "If by some miracle, he did survive. If that truly is Judas in there talking to Mother and Father, engaged to my sister, then what are we going to do?"

"I don't know." Elaine thought the matter over. "But you can't tell them."

"What?" Henry hissed, jerking his chin at the sound of blindsiding his family.

"You cannot say a word," Elaine clarified. "To your mother, to your father, not even to Louisa." Her vibrant green eyes looked like liquid zeal in the light.

"Louisa is engaged to that man," Henry argued, raising his voice. "What on earth do you mean I cannot tell her? In no time at all, she could be his wife!"

"Henry," Elaine scolded. "Lower your voice."

"Elaine, I cannot bear the thought of that man in my parents' house!"

Elaine grabbed his chin and gritted her teeth. "Listen to me. You will not mention one word of this to anyone. Not to your parents and especially not to your sister."

"And why on earth would I do that, Elaine?" Henry growled back at her.

"Because right now, you and I are the only two who know the true identity of that man. Don't you see, Henry? We know his greatest secret. It's the only leverage we have."

Henry stepped away and let his arms dangle at his sides. Whether he would admit it or not, Elaine was right. To play chess with the pirate, they would undoubtedly need the upper hand. But with someone as ruthless as Judas, how long would the advantage last?

"So I am supposed to walk in there and dine with the man who murdered your father, who murdered Jade, who would have murdered you, with a smile on my face?"

Elaine touched his shirtsleeve. "You must act, Henry. Play your part."

Henry jerked his arm from her hold. "Fine. If I must." Fuming with rage at the position Judas had put them in, Henry opened the double doors and bolted out of the drawing room.

\* \* \*

For the next hour, Henry held his tongue as Judas entertained the table with tales of heroic voyages at sea. Elaine took her fork and jostled the food back and forth on her plate, unable to meet his dark blue eyes. Every word that left Judas's mouth could not be mistaken for embellishment in her eyes. Elaine knew the difference between that and a lie.

"I plan to take some time off after Louisa and I are wed." He turned to the lovesick girl by his side and took hold of her hand. "We will honeymoon in Europe: London, Paris, Rome. It is my greatest intention to show her the world."

Louisa blushed until her cheeks were rosy pink. The touch of William's skin to her own filled her entire body with warmth. Of all the promises he had made her, a happy life with William Pierce was the one she looked forward to the most. Perhaps she was young and wholly inexperienced when it came to the intentions of handsome young men. But that was no matter to Louisa. For she was absolutely in love with him.

"I wonder, may I ask your age, sir?" Henry butted in. "How old are you?"

Judas smiled at either of Henry's parents, then turned his focus to Henry.

"Yes," Elaine reiterated. "I was just wondering the same thing myself."

Judas squirmed in his seat and let go of Louisa's hand. After planting his elbows against the tablecloth, he folded his fingers and eyed his glass of wine. "Well, if you must ask," he dragged the phrase out to no avail. "I am twenty-five."

"Really?" Henry set a finger to his lips. "You look much older than that."

"Well, I don't believe one's appearance should be an absolute indicator of age." Judas waved a hand at Elaine. "Take your young wife, for instance. From the look of her, I would assume that she could be no more than sixteen. Wouldn't you say so, Henry?"

Henry's nostrils flared as he made a fist on the

table.

"True," Elaine bluntly remarked. "But I am not sixteen."

Silence fell over the dining room table, as Mrs. Rochester racked her brain for a way to steer the conversation in a new direction. "And what of your wedding plans?" she said. "Won't the ceremony take place in a matter of weeks?"

"Yes." Louisa took William's hand and braided her fingers through his. When she looked into his beautiful blue eyes, she could see the wonderful future ahead of them. Like a breathtaking landscape they would paint together. She wanted to be his wife, his lover, mother to all of his children, no matter how many there might be. "Three long weeks."

Louisa admired her future husband with no shame, returning the cheerful smile that always seemed to be plastered on his face. To her, William Pierce was everything.

"Oh, there is so much joy in the family now," Mrs. Rochester boasted, more of an appreciation of loved ones than an excuse to brag. "First Henry and Elaine give us a beautiful baby girl, our first grandchild. And now Louisa will be wed within a month."

"Grandchild?" Judas echoed. "I was not aware of the new addition to the Rochester family." He lifted his wine glass to Henry and Elaine, though failed to follow through the proper notions of a toast. "Congratulations! I'll bet she is a beautiful baby girl."

As Judas took a sip of wine, Henry pushed his chair out from the table and rose to his feet, fleeing the room before he chose to do anything he might later regret. Marching through the house, he took the stairs two at a time and immediately proceeded into the room occupied by his daughter. Pulsing with rage, he reached the crib and gazed down at sweet Lilly. The sight of her sleeping soundly dissolved his anger at once.

"Forgive my husband," Elaine apologized, excusing his absence downstairs. "With the baby, neither of us have the luxury of a good night's rest anymore."

"Don't mind, Henry," Mr. Rochester said. "It is perfectly fine."

"Thank you." Elaine rose to her feet and held her hands behind her back. "But I would like to speak to my husband and check on our little one. If you'll excuse me."

As Elaine left the room, Judas spoke up in an attempt to delay her departure. "I would like to meet her," he announced, pleased at the sight of Elaine's frozen figure.

She swallowed and glanced back at him. "Who?"

With another sip of wine, Judas smiled. "Why, Elaine, your daughter, of course."

A grin smeared across his face, and it was a wicked one.

Vengeance surged through her veins as Elaine

turned on her heel and followed the path Henry had just taken. Climbing the staircase with a pounding head, Elaine rushed into the guest room and softly shut the door behind her. There she found Henry standing in front of the crib with Lilly protectively cradled in his strong, muscular arms.

"What is he playing at?" Elaine hissed, keeping her voice down.

"I do not know." Henry handed Lilly off to Elaine and headed for the door. "I must speak with Father. Alone in his study. I must warn him of the man his daughter is about to marry."

"No, Henry!" Elaine grabbed his elbow and pulled him back. The action stirred the baby awake as she started to cry. "Do not tell him who William is. You promised!"

"I won't tell him what we know." Henry straightened his coat. "But I am curious. What does Father think of this man? This William Pierce, as he calls himself."

"I wouldn't mind knowing myself." Elaine gently jostled Lilly in her arms as Henry left them alone in the room. When the door closed, Elaine sat down in a rocking chair and held the baby close. She could not bear the thought of Judas touching her child.

\* \* \*

Frantic with nervous energy, Henry made a slow descent down the staircase and refrained from unleashing his temper. Thankful to discover that Mr. Rochester had already retired to his study for the evening, Henry rapped his knuckles against the door and sighed.

"Come in," Mr. Rochester gruffly called, perhaps sensing his son drawing near.

After searching the deserted hallway, Henry opened the door and stepped inside.

"Henry." Mr. Rochester balanced his reading glasses on the end of his nose. "Have a seat, son. And shut the door, why don't you?"

Obeying at once, Henry closed the door and ambled towards the vacant chair across from his father's desk. Once he took a seat, the matter of addressing his father became all the more taxing on his nerves. What could he say to him?

Mr. Rochester set his glasses down on his desk and sighed with sadness. "You know, Henry. When I look back on my life, I remember the birth of you and your sister. Now you have a child of your own, and Louisa has grown into a woman overnight."

"Father, Louisa is sixteen." Henry gripped the edge of his father's desk. "In a sense, that man could practically be her father. Does that not bother you?"

"What can I do about it?" Mr. Rochester questioned. "Louisa is no longer my little girl. She is a woman capable of making her own decisions. William is the man she has chosen."

Henry dragged his upper teeth across his bottom lip. "But Father, what if William is not the man for her?" He leaned in closer. "What if she is choosing wrong?"

Mr. Rochester squared his shoulders and pinned his eyebrows together. Reclining back, he rested his elbows along the arms of his chair and contemplated for a while. He was more curious than ever to learn the essence of Henry's thoughts.

"You disapprove of Mr. Pierce?" Mr. Rochester clipped. "Why?"

Henry braided his fingers together and then released them, flattening his palms side by side. "How much do we even know of the man? He is practically a stranger."

"Henry, tonight is not the first that your mother and I have been in the company of young William. You and Elaine have been occupied with the baby. But I can assure you that we have taken the time to know him. Do you really think I would give my blessing to just anyone? Do you really think I would give him permission to marry my daughter?" Mr. Rochester turned red in the face.

"Father, I have never mistaken you for a fool. Do not think that—"

"William is a good match for your sister. I do not mind the age difference, because he will be a better man to her. He will be able to take on the responsibilities of a husband."

"But Father—"

"Your sister has made her decision and so have I," Mr. Rochester barked. "You will not change my mind, and I doubt you have the capacity to change your sister's either."

Henry looked off, feeling as though he had been backed into a corner.

"I appreciate your concern for your sister, son." Mr. Rochester slipped his glasses back on and watched Henry through the rounded lenses. "But it is most uncalled for."

Hopelessly defeated, Henry accepted the outcome and rose to his feet.

"I expect to see you in the office first thing in the morning, Henry."

"Yes, sir." Henry left the room and closed the door behind him. After lingering in the hallway by himself, Henry heard the sound of Elaine's cry and bolted up the staircase.

## Chapter 4

**E**laine gazed down upon her baby daughter, gently rocking her back and forth in the chair. In time, Lilly calmed to the soothing cadence of her mother's singing voice and drifted off. Relieved to watch her rest, Elaine held the child to her breast and closed her eyes with a taxing sigh. Henry may not admit it, but Elaine was frightened.

Failing to push the darkness away, Elaine stood up with a clouded mind and returned Lilly to her crib. Her pulse thrummed louder with every passing second, as Elaine recalled the dreams, the nightmares, the premonitions. Had she been a fool to ignore the imaginative warnings in her mind? For Judas was back. In true living color.

The door creaked open and Elaine listened, wondering why her visitor did not possess the decency to knock.

"What a charming room," Judas declared. "Do you visit your husband's parents often?"

Gazing down at her sleeping child, Elaine placed her hand on Lilly's chest. Then she lowered her lashes as red hot blood pounded in her eardrums.

"It is a lovely place." Judas took one step forward and then another, holding his hands behind his back. "The home you share with your husband is just as lovely, I imagine."

Elaine kept still with her back turned to him. She knew neither what to do nor say.

Judas grinned at her in silence. "Dear friend. After all this time, have you nothing to say to me?"

"Friend?" Elaine spun around and set her hands on the railing of Lilly's crib. "After everything you've done, how on earth could you possibly call me your friend?"

With a closed mouth, Judas quirked his lips to the side. "Your beauty has yet to fade," he noted. "In fact, I believe the child has only added to it."

Elaine shut her eyes and scowled. "What do you want, Judas? Why are you here?"

Judas hovered closer. "You have something of mine. I want it back."

Unpleasantly anxious, Elaine glowered up at him with a pair of glistening green eyes. "I stabbed you in the heart," she whispered. "I left you there to die. However did you make it off that island?"

Taking her remark as a compliment, Judas reached out and touched his palm to Elaine's cheek. She batted his arm away at the wrist and sneered at him in revulsion. "Such soft skin,"

Judas murmured.

Fuming with rage, Elaine got in his face and glared into his cobalt eyes. "You will never touch me again."

Judas moistened his lips and swallowed. "We shall see about that."

Elaine exhaled through her nostrils, and Judas's eyes flicked to her chest as it rose and fell. "I killed you," she rasped. "When we left the island, you were dead."

Turning to his side, Judas studied the intricate detailing on the bureau before him. "You're awfully wise," he said. "For a woman."

Elaine studied the angle of his jawline, the sharp, strong nature of its appearance. He gritted his teeth and smoldered, looking back at her. For a fleeting moment, Elaine recognized that Judas was beautiful. Evil, yet beautiful.

"How did you survive?" Elaine pressed, holding his predatory gaze without a blink.

"I assume you received my wedding gift." Judas crossed his arms over his chest and took a step too close.

Feeling threatened, Elaine turned her chin up, holding it high and mighty. Blood pulsed through her veins, as she had practically quit breathing. She never felt more uncomfortable than when he was standing in the room.

"There is an old legend from an ancient island tribe," Judas muttered, "that if you cut out the heart of a lion, you will capture its spirit."

Tears filled Elaine's eyes as she declared, "Jade was no lion."

"Perhaps not," Judas agreed. "But close enough."

"What do you want?" Elaine barked. "I have nothing of yours."

Aiming to increase her level of discomfort, Judas reached around her body and set his hand along the railing of the crib. Elaine stilled and swallowed, folding her arms across her chest. As she looked down, all she could feel was the stinging warmth of Judas's breath.

"The treasure is missing, and I know that you have it." Judas gazed down upon her, watching the paralyzing effect he had on her body. "You and your husband."

"I have no idea what you are talking about," Elaine coolly replied.

Wanting her full attention, Judas grabbed her chin until her eyes were on him. "I want that treasure, and I will have it, Elaine. Even if young Louisa must pay the price."

"You wouldn't touch her," Elaine remarked.

"She loves me, island girl." Judas stroked his calloused fingertips along her jawline. "And she will do whatever I ask her to."

"Leave my sister alone," Elaine demanded, though he had never been one to listen.

"She is not your sister," Judas proclaimed. "She is the sister of your husband."

Elaine turned her face away and clenched her

jaw. If not for the newborn child she was shielding behind her, Elaine would have fled the room in pursuit of Henry. Where was he when she needed him?

"Perhaps that is the problem," Judas said. "If Louisa were your own blood..." He stared at sleeping Lilly in the crib. "If she were your own child, perhaps you would behave differently."

Water blurred her eyes as Elaine uttered, "She is an innocent baby."

With the shake of his head, Judas popped the end of his tongue against his teeth. "She is human," he announced. "None of us are innocent."

Judas shoved Elaine out of the way and lunged for her child.

"NO!" Elaine cried, her voice amplifying into a mournful scream.

Henry burst through the door and looked about the room. After discovering the source of conflict, he ran and tackled Judas to the ground. The blade in his hand was now in Henry's, as the latter held it to Judas's throat.

"Do not ever touch my child or my wife again," Henry growled.

Judas curled his lips into a smile, as Elaine rested a hand over her stomach and cried.

"Tell me why I should not cut your throat, right now," Henry commanded.

"Because I wouldn't want to get any blood on that pretty wife of yours."

The remark set Henry off, as he slammed Judas's head into the ground. Having heard the scuffle downstairs, Mrs. Rochester barged into the room with Louisa and Mr. Rochester behind her. They froze in place at the sight of Judas pinned to the floor, petrified with shock.

"Good God, Henry!" Mrs. Rochester shrieked. "What is the matter with you?"

"William," Louisa cried, rushing over to him as Mr. Rochester jerked Henry up off the floor. "Oh, William. Are you hurt?" She looked at the love of her life with a pair of innocent blue eyes while her brother paced the floor and steamed like a bull.

"Yes, my love." William took her delicate face in his big hands and cooed.

"Son, you better have a very good explanation for this," Mr. Rochester declared.

Frantic with fear, Elaine's eyes met Henry's across the room as they exchanged like-minded thoughts without opening either of their mouths. With the scene they had just witnessed, Mr. and Mrs. Rochester would never believe that Elaine or Lilly had been in danger. If anything, Judas would be viewed as the victim and Henry the victimizer.

"It was nothing, sir." William curled his arm around Louisa's back, though it was hardly any trouble to bring her close. Her arms were already twisting around him like a vine.

Mr. Rochester set his hands on his hips and glared at Henry.

"I believe I have overstayed my welcome." William swept his blonde locks out of his face and left a brief kiss on Louisa's cheek. "Good night, my dear Louisa."

When William walked out of the room with a stride as smooth as that of a jungle cat, Louisa watched until the image of him was no more than a memory. "Henry, how could you?" She covered her mouth and wept, casting a resentful glower in her brother's direction.

"Louisa, you don't know what that man is capable of." Henry moved towards her with the intention of wrapping her in his embrace as a sign of comfort. "Stay away from him."

"Stay away from him?" She backed away from Henry and pain flitted across his face in return. "How dare you! How dare you ask me to stay away from the man I love!"

"Louisa!" Henry called after her.

But she sprinted from the room and ran down the staircase, chasing after William and calling out his name. She had spent a lifetime waiting for her true love to appear. Now that he had, nothing would stand in between the two of them. Not even flesh and blood.

Once Mrs. Rochester followed in her daughter's footsteps and shut the door behind them, Mr. Rochester stalked towards Henry and got in his face. "I understand that you do not approve of the man," Mr. Rochester reasoned. "But Henry, your behavior is unacceptable."

Henry held his tongue and brought his golden eyes to his father.

"I am disappointed in you, Henry." Mr. Rochester waved his fist in the air and took to shouting, the vein in his forehead loudly protruding outward. "How could you embarrass your mother and I in front of Louisa's betrothed? After the stunt you just pulled, that man may never step foot in this house again! Have you any compassion for your sister?"

Henry feathered his fingers through his hair and then reached out to grab Mr. Rochester's shoulders. "Father, if you only knew what that man has—"

"Henry, don't!" Elaine warned, her voice firm and desperate.

Mr. Rochester cast a glance in Elaine's direction, then pulled out of Henry's hold. For a moment, he stood their contemplating the matter, wondering if there was some important piece of the puzzle he was missing. But the young Mr. Pierce had won him over from the start, cordial and well-respected and kind. He would be a fool to let his daughter marry any other. So he stood by his original decision, no matter the opinion of Henry or his wife.

Rolling his sleeves up to the elbow, Mr. Rochester gazed at his son out of pity. "Your firstborn has taken a lot out of you, Henry. Why don't you take the day off tomorrow? Stay home with your wife. Spend time with your daughter. I am not asking you, Henry."

Stunned at whose side his father had chosen, Henry stood there gaping when Mr. Rochester walked out of the room and left him alone with Elaine. Rage boiled within him, because Judas had crept his way into the hearts of his father, mother, and young sister. What upset him the most was the fact that all three of them had chosen Judas over him.

They had believed the savage, the killer, the pirate.

But how could Henry blame them?

They didn't know any better.

"I'm sorry, Henry," Elaine whispered, feeling that she had done him an injustice.

Henry turned back to his wife and lowered his eyes. "We're going home."